Dark, billowing clouds raced across the sky.

Vicki had never seen clouds move so rapidly before. They made her uneasy. She gritted her teeth, fighting the sensation of fear.

What was the matter with her? She felt so cold. As if she were treading where she shouldn't be, walking through a graveyard at midnight. She had a strange intuition that she'd crossed some forbidden line. She was seeing things she wasn't meant to see.

Jason reached for her hand. Just as they touched, a tremendous bolt of lightning flashed down nearby. The thunder that rolled and clashed in its wake was instant and alarming.

Vicki looked up. The sky was nearly black. The trees were dipping and swaying, bowed down beneath the strength of the wind. She and Jason ran through the arch created by the lashing trees. A field of electricity snapped and cracked around them. It seemed they ran forever, then burst out into a clearing.

Then Vicki took a look around her, and screamed.

Dear Reader,

This month we welcome you to a new venture from Silhouette Books—Shadows, a line designed to send shivers up your spine and chill you even while it thrills you. These are romances, but romances with a difference. That difference is in the fear you'll feel as you journey with the heroine to the dark side of love . . . then emerge triumphantly into the light. Who *is* the Shadows hero? Is he on the side of the angels? Sometimes. But sometimes neither you nor the heroine can be sure and you wonder, *Does he want to kiss me—or kill me?*

And what a lineup of authors we have for you. This month we're bringing you *four* tantalizing, terrifying titles by authors you won't be able to resist. Heather Graham Pozzessere is known to romance readers everywhere, but in *The Last Cavalier* she demonstrates an ability to spook you that will . . . well . . . haunt you long after you've turned the last page. In *Who Is Deborah?,* Elise Title gives her heroine amnesia, leading her to wonder if the man who claims they are married is telling the truth. Because if he's not, what on earth happened to his real wife? Lee Karr's *Stranger in the Mist* mingles past, present and future into a heady brew that will leave you guessing until the very end. And in *Swamp Secrets,* Carla Cassidy creates one of the darkest—and sexiest!— heroes I've seen in a long, long time.

And that's only the beginning! Because from now on we'll be bringing you two Shadows novels every month, novels where fear mingles with passion to create a reading experience you'll find nowhere else. And the authors who will be penning these books are some of the best anywhere. In months to come you'll find books by Jane Toombs, Helen R. Myers, Rachel Lee, Anne Stuart, Patricia Simpson, Regan Forest and Lori Herter, to name only a few. So now, step into the shadows and open yourself up to romance as you've never felt it before—on the dark side of love.

Yours,

Leslie J. Wainger
Senior Editor and Editorial Coordinator

HEATHER GRAHAM
POZZESSERE

The Last Cavalier

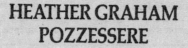SILHOUETTE® *Shadows*™

Published by Silhouette Books New York
America's Publisher of Contemporary Romance

SILHOUETTE BOOKS
300 East 42nd St., New York, N.Y. 10017

THE LAST CAVALIER
Silhouette Shadows # 1

Copyright © 1993 by Heather Graham Pozzessere

All rights reserved. Except for use in any review, the reproduction or utilization of this work in whole or in part in any form by any electronic, mechanical or other means, now known or hereafter invented, including xerography, photocopying and recording, or in any information storage or retrieval system, is forbidden without the permission of the publisher, Silhouette Books, 300 E. 42nd St., New York, N.Y. 10017

ISBN: 0-373-27001-1

First Silhouette Books printing March 1993

All the characters in this book have no existence outside the imagination of the author and have no relation whatsoever to anyone bearing the same name or names. They are not even distantly inspired by any individual known or unknown to the author, and all incidents are pure invention.

® and ™: Trademarks used with authorization. Trademarks indicated with ® are registered in the United States Patent and Trademark Office, the Canada Trade Mark Office and in other countries.

Printed in the U.S.A.

Books by Heather Graham Pozzessere

Silhouette Shadows

The Last Cavalier # 1

Silhouette Intimate Moments

Night Moves # 118
The di Medici Bride # 132
Double Entendre # 145
The Game of Love # 165
A Matter of Circumstance # 174
Bride of the Tiger # 192
All in the Family # 205
King of the Castle # 220
Strangers in Paradise # 225
Angel of Mercy # 248
This Rough Magic # 260
Lucia in Love # 265
Borrowed Angel # 293
A Perilous Eden # 328
Forever My Love # 340
Wedding Bell Blues # 352
Snowfire # 386
Hatfield and McCoy # 416
Mistress of Magic # 450

Silhouette Books

Silhouette Christmas Stories 1991
"The Christmas Bride"
*Silhouette Shadows
Story Collection* 1992
"Wilde Imaginings"

HEATHER GRAHAM POZZESSERE

considers herself lucky to live in Florida, where she can indulge her love of water sports, like swimming and boating, year-round. Her background includes stints as a model, actress and a bartender. She was once actually tied to the railroad tracks to garner publicity for the dinner theater where she was acting. Now she's a full-time wife, mother of five, and, of course, a writer of historical and contemporary romances.

PROLOGUE

Blackfield's Mountain
September, 1862

Before...

The Confederate cavalry officer stood staring down Blackfield's Mountain, his gloved hands upon his hips, his silver-gray eyes fixed on the field that stretched out below him. His uniform sat well upon his broad shoulders and tautly muscled physique. His plumed hat sat low over his brow, concealing from his waiting men any emotion written in his eyes. His looks were striking; his handsomely chiseled features, hardened perhaps by the endless months of war, but arresting nonetheless. They were features that gave a measure of the man—the silver-gray eyes always steady; his mouth generous; his smile quick. He knew how to command, how to be stern, how to be merciful. Best of all, he knew how to instill his men with courage, while also doing his damnedest to keep them all alive.

A spasm of unease suddenly crept along his spine. He commanded the crest of the mountain at the moment, but there was something he didn't like about the day. The air was dry and still, yet curious gray clouds were forming to the east. It was early morning, but already the battlefield was nearly black with the powder from Yankee mortar and Confederate Napoleons. A man could barely see two feet in front of his face.

But Jason Tarkenton had been given the order to charge, and so he would. Jackson was the commanding general, and Jason deeply respected the man. General Jackson made few mistakes.

Cavalry was most often used as reconnaissance, riding ahead, scouting out enemy positions. Then sometimes cavalry met cavalry ahead of the other troops.

Today, both the Yanks and the Rebs were forced to use their cavalry units to fight. They had done so before. Too many times, Jason thought.

For some reason, though, it seemed that this time it was a mistake. But if old "Stonewall" had ordered him to take his troops into the battle, then Jason would do so. Jackson had ordered them to hold the mountain. They would damned well try their very best to do so.

"Now, Jason?"

He arched a brow. His brother, John, anxiously asked him the question. Young, but a damned good military man for his tender age, John stood holding the reins to Jason's big black gelding. After two years of training at West Point, John had been pulled back from the Yankee stronghold to fight the war. His rank was captain and his duties were to serve Jason as aide-de-camp.

In times like this, he never remembered to address Jason in a proper military fashion. But today, Jason just smiled. It didn't seem like the right time to remind anyone about protocol or procedure. Jason gazed at John, then blinked painfully against the oppressive powder and the debilitating heat of the day.

Now. Yes, it should be now.

Still, he hesitated, and wondered if the awful days of endless fighting in Virginia were wearing him down at last. *He didn't dare hesitate! The battle could be lost through hesitation!* What was wrong? He didn't like the day. He just didn't like the day.

Didn't like the day? Since when did he get to choose when the Yankees would attack?

The enemy had been gathering in the valley, definitely preparing to attack. They had to take the initiative!

He gritted his teeth, determined that his brother would not see his unease or his hesitation. He was accustomed to the blinding properties of the black powder created by the cannon fire and the gun shot. He knew the shouts and cries of battle, the screams of dying men and horses. Damn it, he knew how to lead men, how to charge and how to retreat.

Today, things seemed worse. Different. Maybe it was the air, the damned air. It had a feel about it. As if it were charged with more than an earthly fire.

Maybe it was the sky. There seemed to be a promise of rain from the heavens above. The distant clouds that had grown as black as the powder of cannon fire, seemed to billow and roil in a constant, wild action. Yet here, where he stood, the day seemed unbelievably still.

A tempest was coming. A tempest deeper than battle, louder than any clash of steel. It seemed as if God Himself had grown angry with the fratricide, and was about to grumble out his wrath. There was something ethereal about the air. Something tense, something charged with a strange lightning...

Something ghostly...

Jesu! And he was supposed to be a military man!

He pulled down impatiently on his hat, stiffening, and standing very tall in his cavalry officer's yellow-trimmed gray. Hell, it was war! No matter that he faced half his old friends from West Point, no matter that he had once been *U.S.* cavalry himself. He'd been facing old friends on the battlefield since his troops had first entered the fray at Manassas. This was war. *War.* It was natural that a battlefield should be fraught with tension. That it should be *charged.* It was even natural that God should be angry, watching all the men, so many in the flower of youth, bleed, break and die.

Naturally! There was something ghostly about it all. Men were going to die.

And it was time to enter into the fray.

"Now, John," he said quietly, keeping his emotion from his voice.

But it sure did look like suicide. If the Yank shot didn't get them, they might well be gunned down by their own artillery. He turned slightly, looking out over the field of his men. Young and old. Graybeards and green young fellows, all of them a little lean in the face, since they had been with him quite some time now. Some leaned upon their rifles, some just standing by their mounts. With level eyes and infinite faith, they watched him. In silence, they awaited his command. And every man jack there would follow him without question. He lowered his head, smiling. Well, hell, they had their pride. They might all be as stupid as all get-out to go racing into forces that outnumbered them three to one, but it was the courageous thing to do, and that was one thing every Southerner liked to claim—wagonloads of courage. And honor. He mustn't forget that. Young men fell like flies for the honor of dying for their beloved cause.

He was no better!

Again he reminded himself firmly, *It was war!* They had no choice.

Taking the reins from John, he mounted Max, his huge black gelding. Mortar exploded nearby, uprooting a giant oak. A horse screamed, and the powder in the air thickened around them. Max, good old warhorse that he was, remained still, as accustomed to shot and fire as his master.

"Jackson's asked us to keep the mountain, boys!" he told them.

"Yessir!" cried back one of the men.

"Yessir!" was echoed all around.

He pulled down on his hat again. "I'll guess we'll keep the mountain, then!"

Looking back up the mountain, Jason could scarcely see their own artillery. There was a fallen body at his side. A man killed in the earlier fighting. Jason knew that the dead man was an artillery private only by the stripe of red that ran along the side of his uniform trousers. There was nothing else left that could distinguish his identity.

The smoke cleared somewhat. Jason drew his saber from the sheath at his side and raised it high. Some distant ray of sunshine broke through the clouds and powder to touch down upon the blade, and it glinted silver in the air. The Yanks were down there regroup-ing, Jason knew. They were ready to start their own charge up the mountain. It would be far better to meet them in the valley, and leave themselves the top of the mountain for their field of retreat. In the valley, there would be room to maneuver, room to beat back num-bers far greater than their own.

Now.

"Charge!" Jason ordered.

"Yessir!" rose the voices of his men.

He nodded. His saber slashed through the air as he stretched low over his horse's neck, leading the ad-vance.

He felt the hoofbeats pound beneath him, and the vibration of the earth as over a hundred mounts fol-lowed hard behind him. Ahead of him lay the enemy in blue. Men and boys. Some would fall, and some would die. And soon, somewhere, someplace in time, mothers would cry and widows would grieve. And that was what war was: death and despair. But a man was called upon to fight it and it was best not to dwell upon the pain and horror. Better to think about staying mounted, about avoiding the falling shrapnel, about fighting and surviving.

Yet, if he fell . . . Well, how much would it matter? Widows and sweethearts were supposed to weep, and soldiers were supposed to die.

But here he rode, alive and well, while Lydia lay in the cold darkness of the earth, beautiful even in death, so fragile in that beauty.

"Jesu!" Even above the hideous pounding on the earth and the roar of fire, he could hear his brother's cry to heaven as mortar exploded all around them. The earth came up in big chunks and rained back down upon them. Jason looked John's way. It must have been a hundred degrees, and their uniforms were made of wool. Sweat dripped down the lean planes of John's face.

A chorus of shouts rose up behind Jason, loud and strong. The Rebel yell, coming from each of the men who were riding hard down the mountain for their date with destiny and doom.

They charged into the fray.

Jason lost all track of himself. He met Union steel with his Richmond saber and fought and hacked and fought again. The cavalry troops began the battle; they were quickly joined on the field by the infantry, running behind with their own Rebel yell.

All around him, horses and men screamed. Men in blue and gray. Cannons continued to bellow, guns to roar.

Jason stared into faces. Young faces. Faces of boys still wet behind the ears. Faces that would never age enough to bear more than a pale wisp of peach fuzz. Faces that were gnarled with years, gray whiskered, leathered. He couldn't choose between the faces. Kind faces, hard faces, gentle faces. This was war, so he must battle. When a sword raised to his, he fought for his own life, and shoved back any thoughts of an easier, gentler time when he might have shared a whiskey with any one of these Yanks in some nameless tavern upon a nameless road.

The smoke was awful. The day grew grayer. Darker. What little light there was, reflected in the blood spilled upon the earth.

The Confederate troops gained an advantage, and a retreat was sounded for the Union soldiers.

"*Jason!* We've done it!" John shouted, waving his arm. His horse pranced at a small distance from Jason's. "They're skedaddling, those blue bellies!"

"Look at them run!" cried Henry Ostraw, another of his men.

Jason shook his head with both impatience and sorrow. *Let them go. Let's all live!* his heart cried. But he was an officer. He couldn't let the Yanks regroup and come after them again. "Give chase!" he commanded.

His bugler began to sound out the order on the dark and dusky air. Jason waved his sword in a circle, and cried the order again. "Give chase!" Then he nudged Max's thighs, and the animal sprang forward, lunging into a gallop, racing after the enemy who was already disappearing into the forest at the base of the valley.

Suddenly, there was a roar of cannon, and his brother screamed. Jason saw that John was no longer riding at his side. He raised a hand to Lieutenant Nigel Keefe, his second in command, indicating that he should lead the men on forward. Nigel and his troops obeyed, racing onward into the darkening day.

Jason reined in Max, carefully trotting back, scarcely able to see in the red-and-gray day. He heard a moan, and only then saw John on the ground before him. He hastily dismounted, falling to his knees beside his brother. It was John's arm that had been hit. Shrapnel. The arm was badly ripped up. The bone had been shattered.

The surgeons would amputate, and hell, it seemed that infection always set in after an amputation, and then...

And then a man died.

Not my brother, damn it all to hell! He looked to heaven, both fury and agony in his heart. He'd lost too damned much already. Not John. He wouldn't lose John, too!

John was bleeding, bleeding badly. Jason quickly pulled his mustard scarf from about his throat and applied it as a tourniquet to John's arm. "It's going to be all right," he assured his brother. "I've just got to get a surgeon and—"

"Hell, no!" John protested. "Ah, hell, Jason, it's bad, really bad, and I'm not any man's fool. I'm going to die. Let me go easy, Jason. Don't let those old sawbones chop me up before I go."

"Now, dammit, John. You aren't going to die. I'm not going to let you die." Brave words. He had to get help. Despite the tourniquet, John was still bleeding badly.

But men were bleeding all over the battlefield. Men were dying all over the battlefield. The surgeons, orderlies and nurses were already out, attending to the wounded. They weren't alone. Some wives and lovers, camp followers, even some of the braver local population, were out, too, doing their best to tend to the wounded, to sort the living from the dead.

And seeing to the fallen men in blue, as well as the men in gray.

Jason gritted his teeth. Someone would be along. He had always prided himself on being such a damn good military man. He should turn away from John and ride on to lead his men.

But in the midst of all this suffering, something had to matter. In all the sacrifice and horror—in the great quest for honor—something still had to matter.

John mattered.

"Listen to me, John. You aren't going to die. Hell, I can't fight this stinking war without you! Ma would be rolling over in her grave right now, crashing into Pa! I can't let you go, John. I can't. Don't you dare die on me. The two of them will haunt me the rest of my days!"

As he'd hoped, he drew a painful smile from his brother.

"Now, I'll be right back. You just lie there, nice and still. In case we should start to lose this ground again, shimmy your way under that rock. You don't want to wind up injured in a Yank camp, right?"

John nodded at him bleakly. "You gotta lead the war, Colonel," John reminded him.

"Oh, so you do know my rank?" He was still trying to keep his voice light. "Keefe knows what he's doing. The war will wait for me for just a few minutes, I'm certain."

John tried to give Jason a thumbs-up signal, but pain was naked in his glazed gray eyes. He was just a kid, Jason thought. Barely twenty. That was war. War killed dreams and slaughtered the future!

Sometimes Jason just wished to hell he could walk away from all of it. Just up and walk away. Disappear.

He whistled for Max, and Max obediently came. Quickly Jason mounted his horse again. "You're going to make it!" he told John. He swung Max around, dug his heels in and leaned low against the gelding's neck to race hard with the gray-and-crimson day once again, trying to catch up to his own lines this time.

Jason swore when another cannon shot exploded right in front of him. The air was so thick with the explosion of powder and earth that he couldn't see a damned thing. He blinked and spoke out loud to Max. "Fools! Can't they keep from shooting at their own damned side?"

He reined in, feeling Max's power beneath him as the gelding pranced, waiting for the powder to settle and for light to break through the darkness. A wind had risen with that burst of cannon. A strange wind. One that seemed to come from both the east and the west.

No, the wind didn't come from the east and the west, especially not when the day had been dead calm just a few minutes ago. Dead calm, with a leaden gray sky.

But despite the strange wind, the powder swirl that had filled the air did not settle. It seemed to grow. Odd. There was a loud crack in the sky, like the sound of a cannon, but distinctly *not* the sound of a cannon.

He stared skyward. Clouds, billowing black and gray, seemed to rush down toward him. He threw out an arm in defense—in defense against a *cloud?*—and watched in amazement. There was an arbor of large oaks just to his side. Huge trees that reached the clouds themselves, their branches forming an archway. The clouds billowed and roiled. They curled back into themselves, puffing and swirling there in the archway formed by the swaying branches of trees. He realized with amazement that a strange doorway had been created in the arbor, in the blowing clouds and mist.

All around him strange winds rose, and in their whistling gust he heard a mournful wail, a cry that seemed to echo from the very heart of the dark, twisting heavens. The lashing branches moved like gigantic bony arms, mocking him, beckoning him closer, into their skeletal embrace. And as he watched, an unearthly sensation swept over his body from head to toe, as if someone—or something—was touching him. Touching him with clammy fingers that marked a chilling path down the length of his spine.

The sounds of battle grew dim, as if the fighting were taking place in the far-off distance—as if he heard no more than a memory of those sounds.

Max snorted. "Easy boy," Jason assured him, but he got no farther. His well-trained mount reared and screamed in sudden panic.

As if Max, too, had felt those damp, icy fingers on his flesh....

"Max!" Jason said more firmly, keeping his seat. But then, to his astonishment, his well-trained warhorse bucked and reared again with the violence of a wild stallion. Unprepared for such behavior from Max and half-hypnotized by the strange clouds, Jason reacted too slowly. He was thrown clear and far from the horse, so far that he couldn't even see the animal.

"Max, you son of a mule!" Jason swore as his backside hit the earth. "Max, you get over here!"

The horse whinnied. It seemed as if the sound was coming from very far away.

Jason couldn't see a thing. He pushed up from the ground, rising. He stuck his arms out into the black mist, trying to feel something ahead. He started to walk carefully. John was back there somewhere, but Jason didn't have the time to wait for whatever the hell this was to blow off. He had to keep walking.

The trees! There they were, ahead of him. The trees where the clouds had created a shadowy passage through the darkness and the mist. He had to reach them.

The wind picked up violently. He didn't need to walk toward the trees anymore; he was being swept there.

Fingers! he thought wildly for a moment. Yes, it was as if the bony fingers of some huge, unnatural hand reached for him, dragged him forward. He gritted his teeth, trying with all his strength to push against the funneling winds. But those fingers had captured him in their damp, bone-chilling grip. It was like living a nightmare, feeling himself suspended in time, trapped in the twisting darkness of this unearthly tempest. The winds howled around him like the mournful voices of lost souls, their chill screams and babbling curses hanging in the air.

He was a soldier in Lee's great Army of Northern Virginia! he reminded himself, shaking off the feelings. He had to be afraid of Yankee guns and sabers, and he had to rage against any strange winds that stood in his way.

John. He had to help his brother.

Keep moving!

But even as he moved, the earth itself seemed to shift beneath his feet. Then all of a sudden it was as if he'd walked into a brick wall. He veered back, tripped and started to roll.

"Damnation!" he muttered. Bony fingers be damned, tempests be damned, with his luck, he'd tumble right into a Yank troop. But he couldn't seem to stop himself. He was rolling and rolling and rolling. Mist and clouds and black winds surrounded him.

Wicked, damp, bony fingers seemed to push him right along. He moved faster. The blackness swallowed him. He was a part of it now, he thought. He reached out desperately for a hold to stop himself.

His head hit a rock, and he saw stars. The trees! He had come between them; he was rolling beneath the arbor or the branches that touched the skies, they, too, with long, bleached white, bony fingers that seemed to reach and stroke and scratch at the sky.

Later, he opened his eyes. For a moment, he lay still, his fingers entwined in the rough grass on the earth. He was still on the mountaintop, he thought. He hadn't gone so very far.

And yet, things were different. The blackness was gone. All gone. As if he had blinked it away. He pushed up and looked at the grass and dirt his fingers clutched. The tall grass was deep green, the earth, brown. The air fresh and sweet smelling. He looked up. The sky was a vivid blue, and the sun was blazing golden, high above him. He could hear a whistling, but no eerie moans, no sounds of battle.

"What the bloody hell is going on?" he muttered aloud. Had he been unconscious so very long? He had thought that he'd barely blacked out, just seconds, from the pain.

He started to rise, but then he heard someone calling out, and he ducked low again. Staring downhill through the long grasses, he could see row after row of tents. Army issue, Union tents. Cooking fires blazed away between the tents and delicious aromas rose from the pots hanging over them.

Then there were clusters of tripods created by angled guns. And there were stacks of supplies piled high beside the tents—blankets, tack, burlap sacks.

And there were people. Men and women.

The women were in simple cotton dresses; few seemed to be wearing many petticoats. They were well dressed for army-camp life. The men were in blue. Yankee-issue blue.

Jason pressed his palm against his temple. Damn, there were lots of them! It seemed that he had stumbled into the main portion of the Union army!

Quickly Jason crawled behind a large boulder and leaned his back against it. He closed his eyes. How had he come here? And just where the hell *was* here? How could he have left the mist and blackness so very far away?

How could he have left the battle, the screams for this? The deep green and rich brown of the earth was fresh and sweet smelling. He looked up. The sky was a vivid blue, and the sun was glazing golden, high above him.

CHAPTER ONE

Blackfield's Mountain

Now...

"I tell you, it was very nearly the worst move old Stonewall made during the entire war!"

Liam Douglas's blue eyes were ablaze beneath his shocking white brows and his gnarled old fist made a startling smacking sound against the rough wood table.

Vickie poured more draft into Milt Mahoney's stein and watched a little anxiously as her grandfather drew breath for a reply to Liam. "Jackson was the best general the Confederacy ever had, and Lee damned well knew it!"

Gramps was just as vehement as Liam. His great fist thundered against the table and his eyes crackled with the same blue fire beneath brows as white and bushy as Liam's. The difference between the two octogenarians, Vickie decided, was that Liam had a few strands of hair left, while Gramps was as bald as a buzzard.

"I say that Jackson made one hell of a mistake here!" Liam insisted.

Vickie decided that it was time for her to step into the discussion. "Boys, boys, *boys,* now!" She swooped into the midst of them, giving both Gramps and Liam refills on their beer. She smiled sweetly at all six of the old men filling her grandfather's tiny establishment and reminded them, "The war ended quite some time ago, you know! Well over a hundred years ago now! It was *1865*, remember?"

Liam grinned sheepishly; Gramps looked disgruntled. His kepi was askew on his bald head and despite the air-conditioning in the little tavern, he was sweating. This was a big week for the small Virginia farming town. Not only would the battle itself be reenacted on Saturday, but already, some of the largest reenactment encampments ever drawn together were being set up out in Miller's cornfield right alongside the mountain. Everyone in town was involved in the reenactment in some way. Even those bored by history were entranced by the money-making possibilities stretching before them.

Of course, Gramps had always been a major-league Civil War buff, just like Liam. And therefore, she thought, so was she.

Gramps had gleefully decided that with all the tourists in town, they should dress just like the reenactors. So there he sat, in a Virginia militia field-artillery uniform, while she was walking around serving coffee and beer, dressed in a long antebellum dress. Gramps wanted to get the folks into the spirit of the festivities when they came in for their sandwiches and drinks, and this was the way to do it, he had decided.

She had refused point-blank at first—Gramps's passions got to be a bit too much for her at times—but then he had looked at her so mournfully that she had changed her mind. Gramps's business included an artifacts shop as well as the tavern, and there were times when it felt as if she'd had the history of the place up to her teeth.

But she loved Gramps. He was her only living relative. He'd been there for her when Brad had been killed. Gramps had been her only strength. While she still had the dear old man in her life, she was going to do her best to cherish him. He had wanted her in the dress and petticoats, and she could handle that. But she'd drawn the line at the pantalets and corset. There was no way she was crawling into that part of the costume, and he'd better think good and hard about it! Who was ever going to know what she wore beneath the dress?

Gramps had conceded, but it seemed that she had gained a small victory now. Her russet hair was clumped into a net at her nape and she was dying to set it free, just as she was dying to rid herself of the hot layers of her calico gown.

Glancing up at the clock, she saw that the afternoon was gone. She had promised Karen and Steve that she would come down to the Union camp and see them for dinner. Had she told them six? It was almost six now.

The discussion among the old men had picked up again. They had moved on to the battle of Gettysburg. Vickie politely interrupted them. "Do you need me anymore, Gramps?"

"What? Uh, no, honey. You can run on out and see your friends." He hesitated and added gruffly, "You still going to the Yankee camp?"

She had to laugh, setting a kiss upon his bald head. "Gramps, once again! The war ended, remember?" She set her hands upon his shoulders, lowering her head to whisper in his ear. ''And I hate like hell to tell you this, but they did win, you know!'' She heard his grunt, then rose, winking at his comrades.

Liam snickered and Gramps offered her the ghost of a smile.

''If I were you, young lady,'' Milt warned her, ''I'd take that little filly of yours rather than a car. They aren't letting any cars into the fields where the tents are pitched. Since they have a bunch of the historical-society types coming in with their cameramen and all, they're trying to make everything look just as authentic as possible. You'll have to park way down the road, and you'll have a long, long walk!''

''Thanks for the suggestion, Milt,'' Vickie told him, glad to receive the information. She wasn't really all that far from the encampments, and Arabesque could certainly use the exercise.

She kissed her grandfather again. '''Night, Gramps.''

''Don't you fraternize with them Yankees too long,'' Liam teased.

''I promise not to divulge any military secrets,'' she added with a grin.

Vickie passed from the taproom into the entryway of the old house. She intended to go up to her room and change, but then she paused at the stairway and shrugged. Karen and Steve were very taken up by the make-believe of the whole event. She would stay dressed just as she was.

Gramps's house was old, far older than the Civil War. The carved stairway had been there since the late 1700s, and a tall man could barely walk through some of the doorframes. The foundation for the house had been laid in the late 1600s. It had been a tavern on and off for almost three hundred years.

In the dim light in the entryway she caught sight of her reflection in the wavery hallway mirror. She realized she definitely looked the part that Gramps had asked her to play. Her hand was against her throat and her full skirts were standing out and a web of net still held the bulk of her nearly waist-length hair. Called a day dress, her simple cotton gown had a high-buttoned bodice and a small frill of lace along the wrists, neckline and hem. It was pretty, though, and the dark colors of the plaid went well with her deep auburn hair and bright blue eyes. Gramps had ordered the dress for her from a company that produced the historically accurate uniforms the "soldiers" wore for the reenactments.

She shrugged at her reflection, thinking that the full skirts were actually flattering to her long legs and slim waist. Maybe she'd been unfair to resent the costume all day. "Let's get into the spirit of this thing!" she chastised her mirror image.

Going out the front of the house, she walked around to the rear of the old barn outside and into the stables.

Of the ten stalls, only two were in use, one by Dundee, the other by Arabesque. Vickie had bought Arabesque when she had first come home. Arabesque was a beautiful Arabian mare with a deep "dish" nose, the most beautifully cream-colored mane and tail, and softest bay body that Vickie had ever seen. In the deep and painful confusion that had haunted her after Brad's death, Vickie had learned to appreciate her investment. She had once believed she would never be able to truly accept what had happened. But roaming the endless blue and green fields and forest of the Virginia countryside on the sweet, spirited creature had allowed Vickie to come to a certain peace. She loved the mare.

Vickie slipped a bridle over the horse's nose, led her from her stall, and decided that no one could possibly be looking and made a less-than-ladylike leap onto the mare's sleek, bare back.

Heading northward, she gave Arabesque free rein, delighting in the cooler air that was coming with the setting of the sun. Summer had been viciously hot. Only the evenings gave a slight respite.

She slowed to skirt a neighbor's cornfield, then raced across a barren plain again, climbed over the mountain, and at last saw the endless rows of authentically reproduced Civil War tents that stretched all along the cornfields. Yanks to the west, Rebels to the east, and all manner of sutlers, or salesmen of various goods, were set up in between. Vickie reined Arabesque to a standstill. There was really something special about the scene. The giant Coca-Cola truck—which had been parked there all through the long, hot afternoon by the sutlers' stands—was long gone, as was the big semi that had hauled in Porky's Big Pit Barbecue. The sun was almost down. The horizon gleamed gold and pink over the few sentries who packed corncob pipes and leaned against wooden fences. A lone fiddler, silhouetted in the waning light, played a soft and mournful tune.

"It really is rather beautiful, Gramps," she said softly.

Vickie nudged Arabesque and picked her way down the mountain and through the trails within the cornfields. She came upon the fiddler who had been joined by a young man with a harmonica. She smiled, listening to them. "Pretty tune," she said at last.

The fiddler, a young man with warm brown eyes and hair, smiled back. "Pretty lady," he replied softly.

Her smile deepened. "Thanks. Could you tell me where I could find the 5th Pennsylvania Artillery, Company B?" she asked him then.

The soldier gave Arabesque a pat on her silky neck. He saluted, tipping his kepi to her. "Straight on down the line here," he advised her. "You can't miss them. They've a big flag out with their insignia on it."

"Thanks again. And good night."

"G'night, ma'am."

She idly walked Arabesque down the line, then noticed the flag for the 5th Pennsylvania Artillery just a few tents up ahead.

"Victoria!"

"Steve!" she cried delightedly.

Vickie slid off Arabesque and ran forward to meet the tall slim man with the slightly graying beard who had called her name. He picked her up off her feet, twirled her around, and set her at arm's length from himself. "You're looking good, Vickie, real good! The country air must agree with you!"

She shrugged. "Coming home is always good for the spirit, I think."

He smiled at her warmly. "It's a really beautiful place to come home to. I'm enjoying it tremendously here."

"Vickie!" Karen, Steve's wife, came running around the tent, with her dimpled face aglow, green eyes flashing, and braided blond hair flying. Vickie hugged her friend enthusiastically, then pushed away from her. At first she had thought that Karen had put on a little weight. But the hug had allowed her to realize that Karen was pregnant!

"Oh, you didn't tell me!" Vickie chastised. Then she added quickly, "Congratulations! How very wonderful! Oh, Karen! Are you sure you should be out here like this in your condition?"

"Vickie! I'm pregnant, not sick!" Karen assured her with a laugh. "Besides, Steve has a phone in his car and I'm not due for over three months. I'm fine. Promise."

"Fine enough to sleep in a tent?" Vickie asked, looking from one to the other of the pair.

"I'd sleep anywhere with Steve," Karen assured her, taking her husband's arm affectionately.

"Sure! Make me the heavy!" he moaned, but his gaze upon his wife was very tender. For the first time in a long time, Vickie felt the jagged edge of pain and loss sweep through her. She gritted her teeth, forcing her smile to stay in place. She could remember love like that.

"Come on," Karen said, blissfully unaware of her friend's heartache. "Let me introduce you around."

A number of Steve's fellows from the company were already milling around, jockeying to be close to the newcomer. Vickie was complimented on her gown and her horse, and then on her eyes. At that point, Karen told them all to behave and led Vickie to the cooking pot where she looked down with a mournful expression at some very pathetic vegetables.

"Made from a historically accurate recipe—but not exactly gourmet," Karen warned her. Vickie laughed.

"I don't care what I eat, as long as I eat with friends!" she teased her.

Karen flashed her a quick smile. "Yes, well, thanks to that big lunch I had from Porky's Barbecue, I'm able to agree. Look at this stuff—yuck!"

"Well, I suppose it's authentic."

Karen shoved an onion around with a large wooden spoon. "Maybe it doesn't taste as bad as it looks," she suggested hopefully.

"Maybe... Then again, I should have had the two of you up to the tavern. Gramps makes the meanest chili you've ever tasted this side of the Rio Grande."

"Torture! Torture!" Karen said, shaking her head. "Odd, how I just have a craving for chili at this moment. Well, we'll survive."

Dinner really wasn't so bad. Steve was in with a nice group of guys. One of his friends, Jerry Svenson, told her that the company was made up of New Yorkers, Pennsylvanians and Ohioans. They came from all walks of life, and tried to meet at least three times a year to decide which reenactments, battles and encampments they were going to do each year. "We're actually an open lot," he told her. "Some of the companies—North and South—are made up of men who hail from the same town, and had ancestors in the exact same companies in the real war. Real bunches of good old boys! They fight the war over and over again, as if it were still real. Fanatics."

She smiled, enjoying the cool breeze. "My grand-father is one of those 'good old boys,'" she told him.

"Oh, sorry! I didn't mean—"

"It's all right. And it is funny sometimes. They all had ancestors who actually fought right here, and be-lieve me, they almost come to blows over who made the mistakes!"

"It's easy to become overly involved!"

His words were no sooner out than voices rose around them. Someone was arguing that Ulysses S. Grant had been no better than his predecessors—he had just come around with more men and supplies when Lee's men had just been too decimated and dog-tired to fight anymore.

The reply was quick and furious. Grant had been a damned good general—at the very least, he'd quit re-treating.

Vickie smiled. She realized that she was having a good time. She also realized that Steve and Karen were trying very hard to make sure that she had a good time, and that was why they had invited her here. There were a few other wives around like Karen, who had joined their husbands in the reenactment. But the company was mainly male, and Vickie was definitely receiving a fair share of masculine attention.

And Jerry was pleasant. He was a single stockbro-ker with nice brown eyes and a deep, rich baritone voice.

Vickie just wasn't in the market.

"Where did you meet Steve and Karen?" he asked her.

"My husband and Steve started off in school to-gether. We've been friends for years."

He frowned at the word *husband*. Karen was calling her, and Vickie decided not to enlighten Jerry as to her widowed status. She grinned, excused herself and hurried to Karen. The marshmallows Karen had tried to roast had turned to charred globs of glue.

Vickie laughed, trying to get Karen started again. "I give up!" Karen moaned. She watched Vickie as Vickie reset the sticks to go over the fire. "So how do you like Jerry?"

"He's very nice." She handed the sticks to Karen. "Now toast them—don't melt them."

But Karen ignored the marshmallows.

"Vickie, I know how deeply in love you and Brad were. But he's been dead a long time now. And I'm beginning to think that you're burying yourself down here—"

"I'm not," Vickie assured her quickly, squeezing her friend's hand. "I don't intend to mourn forever and ever . . . honest. It's just that I had the right thing once. If the right thing comes around again, I'll know it."

"But, Vickie, you'll never know—"

"And honestly, Jerry is very nice. I enjoyed his company. And I'll be back. I'll see you tomorrow. Tomorrow the public is allowed in and visit the camps, right? I'll come and sit with you for a while." She wrinkled her nose and deepened her accent, addressing the group. "Besides, I promised Gramps that I wouldn't spend too much time with any damned Yanks!"

"Leave if you have to—but don't forget, you promised us chili, right?" Karen laughed, and let her go. Steve came along, leading Arabesque. Vickie thanked him and mounted the horse. Again she waved a cheerful good-night to all of Company B, and turned Arabesque around to retrace her steps back home.

Salutes and waves and the warmth of campfires followed her at first. But she hadn't gone very far before she realized that she had truly left the light of civilization behind her to ride into the darkness. Once she was away from the glow of those fires, the night seemed stygian.

She was well accustomed to the country, but this night seemed exceptionally dark. There was no moon above to light her way. She reined in on Arabesque and looked back to the camp, suddenly seized by an eerie feeling of impending danger.

"How can I be afraid here?" she mocked herself out loud. But it was dark. So damned dark.

And no matter what she told herself, a feeling of unease had taken root inside her.

Arabesque seemed uneasy, as well. She suddenly whinnied, and then reared high. A night breeze picked up, strong and wild. The horse reared again.

"What—" Vickie began.

There was a blur in the darkness. A figure leapt from behind a rock with such speed that it seemed to swoop down upon her like the wings of a giant bird.

Vickie shrieked in terror as Arabesque reared wildly again, nearly pitching over backward. Vickie was a good rider, but she was bareback in her ridiculous long gown. She lost her grip. Crying out again, she was catapulted to the ground. She hit it hard.

Dazed, she heard a voice. A deep, soft masculine voice with a definite Virginia slur to it. "Whoa, whoa, there!" the voice from the darkness said, soothing

Arabesque. For a moment Vickie remained where she was, too stunned to be frightened, but then she heard the tremor of hoofbeats against the earth as Arabesque went racing away in fear. She heard a mumbled intonation of fury from the man, and then she tried to rise. Her head was splitting. What was the idiot doing?

"You stupid fool!" she hissed irately, but she was quickly silenced. Rough hands held her by the shoulders, dragging her to her feet. Her head still spinning, she stared up into a pair of fierce, blazing, silver-gray eyes that loomed out of the darkness, and a face that was taut with tension.

She knew that she should be afraid. But the fear didn't sink in quite yet. She was staring at him, realizing that he was very handsome. All the planes and angles of his face were lean and strong and nicely sculpted. The nose was straight and the mouth, full and sensual.

"Shush!" he warned her.

"Don't you dare shush me!" Vickie protested loudly. She noticed his cavalry hat then, and the large sweeping plume that protruded from it. His uniform was gray wool with yellow trim. Southern cavalry. Damned authentic, right down to the dust and gunpowder marks. She wasn't sure about the insignias on his uniform. What was he? A colonel?

What difference did it make? It was all pretend.

And he had just caused her to be thrown. In fact, she could have been killed. "Why, you incredible lout! You—" she lashed out again.

A hand clamped over her mouth again. She started to struggle but she suddenly found herself held tightly in his arms, and she felt the deep simmering fire of the silver in his eyes as they stared warningly down into hers. "Sorry, ma'am. But you aren't going to get me caught!"

Caught? Wasn't he taking this playacting just a bit too seriously? What kind of a lunatic was this man?

She twisted, kicking him in the shin. She was furious, but panic was beginning to seize hold of her and she knew she had to act quickly. He grunted in pain and she cast back her head to scream again.

But she never managed to do so. His reflexes were incredibly fast and his hand was over her mouth again so quickly that she didn't manage to emit a single sound. "Shush, and I do mean shush, this time!" he warned her sharply. "All that I wanted was your horse, but I've lost that now. I really don't mean you any harm but I will be damned before I'll let any Yankee-loving whore get me tossed into a prison camp for the duration of this war!"

Her eyes widened incredulously and she was suddenly fueled by her fury again.

Enough was enough. She jerked hard, freeing herself from his grasp. She cracked her hand across his face with all her fury, and opened her mouth, not sure if she meant to scream or tell him exactly what she thought of him.

But it didn't matter. She never managed to do either. Suddenly he had dipped low and butted her belly with his shoulder, throwing her over his back. The air was knocked clean from her. She couldn't even breathe.

Then he was running, with her weight bearing him down, up the mountain. Dazed, Vickie realized that if she managed to scream now, it wouldn't do her a single bit of good. She was too far away from the encampment and heading for the trees that rimmed the crest of the mountain. No one would hear her if she did scream.

The panic she had fought now swept violently through her and she clamped down hard on her jaw as she thudded against his shoulder and back. She desperately sought some logical reason or thought. This had to be some kind of a joke. Steve and Karen had put this man up to this and had arranged it with others in their company. They were probably roaring with laughter right now. She could just imagine Karen innocently teasing her tomorrow. "Well, we thought that maybe a *Rebel* soldier would do the trick, since we Yanks didn't seem to be quite what you wanted...."

Yes, it had to be a trick.

Because if it wasn't, a maniac was dragging her up a mountain, and into an endless trail of forest and deep green darkness.

High atop the mountain, her captor stopped at last. He dropped her down upon the grass and retreated a couple of steps. She could barely see him in the darkness, but at least he was gasping now. Gasping desperately for breath. With some satisfaction, Vickie realized that it had exhausted him to carry her straight uphill for all that distance.

Served him right.

She stood up. She was frightened, but she was still so angry that she only had to swallow once for the courage to speak.

"All right, all right!" she told him. "Cute. Fine, fun. I'm laughing. It was great. What a performance. But now, if you'll just excuse me—"

"You're not going anywhere," he said, interrupting her softly. Yet despite the quiet tone of his words, she felt a shiver snake along her spine. He meant them.

"I'm going where I damned well please!" she informed him, desperately determined that bravado would get her out of this. She whirled around. "Watch me!"

She started walking in the direction from which they had come, her arms swinging, her strides long. But despite her speed, she had barely gotten anywhere before he was upon her. She hadn't heard him move! Hadn't heard a thing. There had just been the slightest whisper of air, and then she was flying. In his arms, and flying.

She landed hard on her backside with the handsome but maniacal stranger straddling over her.

"I told you, I really don't want to hurt you!" he said, catching her chin between his thumb and forefinger. "But you came out of the Union camp," he said, bending closer. She saw the startling tension in his strong features, the fire in his eyes. "I'll be damned a thousand times over before I'll be turned in by a little redheaded witch!"

She stared at him for a long moment, shaken, and yet still furious. What was going on? Who would carry out a joke like this for so long? Was he mad?

But he didn't look mad. He looked just like a soldier, one weary and accustomed to battle, strong and determined. Not cruel, but needing to survive.

There was no war now! It had ended well over a hundred years ago! He was striking, he was unique, but he was either halfway—or all the way!—insane, or else going way too far with this reenactment business.

She stared at him a long moment and then exploded. "I have had it! I mean, I have had it! Okay, okay, I know that some of you guys really get into this thing, but I have really had it. Enough is enough. Now you listen, and listen good. You let me up. You let me up right this second, or so help me God, I will press charges against you for kidnapping and battery!"

A tawny brow hiked up into a curious arch over one of his sizzling silver eyes. "Charges! Charges! Oh, ma'am, I think not! You may be cottonin' up to the Feds here, lady, but this is still the great state of Virginia, and you're addressing a colonel in the Army of Northern Virginia. If any charges are going to be levied, I'll be the one leading those charges!"

"You are an idiot!" she accused him. He seemed really amused now. He didn't trust her in the least but he didn't seem to like the look of her one bit. But with his hard thighs straddled around her hips and his fingers pinning her wrists to the ground, she had nothing to fight with but words. "A fool!" she cried. "Get off of me! If you want to file charges, file charges—"

"Not tonight, I'm afraid. Not tonight!" Once again, his voice was soft. It carried the same chilling determination. "I'm afraid that neither of us is going anywhere tonight."

She felt his silver eyes, pinning her to the ground as strongly as the powerful heat of his touch. "What do you think you're doing!" she cried.

"Surviving," he replied, his gaze steady. "I've got to make it back. I've got to. I've got an injured man waiting for me."

"Who's injured? Tell me, maybe I can—"

"No Yankee help!" he said angrily. He shifted his weight, and she tried with every ounce of her strength to escape him then, but it didn't matter. He rolled her to her stomach and caught her wrists behind her back. He held them there and she screamed aloud in an absolute panic when she heard the fabric at her hem ripping away.

"I'm not going to hurt you!" he reiterated impatiently. "If you would just please shut up!" Apparently he didn't intend to hurt her at the moment, but he didn't intend to let her go, either. He was binding her wrists together with the fabric from her own gown.

Tears stung her eyes. She tasted the dirt and grass from the mountaintop.

She began to seethe and swear furiously against him. Whoever he was, he was the lowest form of life she'd ever encountered in all her years. "You are an incredible idiot, a madman—oh, my God, I can't think of anything ill enough to call you! Bastard, slime, fool, madman—"

His head lowered down to hers against the ground. She felt his husky whisper against her ear, and heard his words, deep, masculine, warning. "I'm going to ask you once, lady. Please quit."

"You're nothing but a petty criminal!" she cried. Oh, God, she hoped that he was petty! What did he intend? "A snake in the grass, the most incredible ass—!"

"Enough!" he warned her.

"No!" she shrieked. "It's not enough. You've got to let me go—"

She heard fabric ripping again. He rolled her back to face him again and she realized that he'd pulled off another good swatch of her hemline. "No!" she cried, staring into his eyes. And he stared back, with those haunting silver eyes, with his disturbingly handsome and set features, and shook his head slowly. The barest curve of a smile turned his lips. "I'm sorry. I've got to get through the night." For a moment she was still, staring into his face. It seemed that he was so very haggard, so very war weary. It seemed as if he really was sorry, as if he didn't want to hurt her. But it also seemed as if he would have his way.

"No—"

The swatch of cloth was bound around her mouth. She shook her head wildly, fighting his touch. She stared at him then, fighting the tears that stung the backs of her eyes. It seemed that he was real. . . .

But he couldn't be. She had been bound and gagged by a madman on the mountain crest. She was nearly helpless. He would hurt her now. . . .

But he didn't touch her again. He straddled over her without a hand on her. He stared back at her, watching her, maybe a little amused, definitely very exasperated. Once again, she thought that he seemed ridiculously real in his uniform. She'd seen so many of those that belonged to the reenactors, and this one was authentic to the last detail. He was so striking in his person with his neck-length tawny hair, silver glinting eyes, lean cheeks, square jaw and hard, set features.

"Woman," he said very softly, "do you ever shut up?" Obviously, he wasn't waiting for an answer. "Go to sleep now," he commanded.

He rose, a tall, tautly muscled man, a powerful figure, standing over her. A man with eyes that blazed a definite strength and warning.

Sleep!

He turned away, and left her.

Sleep!

Oh, no, she would never, never sleep. Never. She was alone on a mountaintop with a maniac, bound and gagged. Her heart was pounding mercilessly, and she was terrified.

He hadn't hurt her. Not yet!

He didn't hurt her. Time passed. He came nowhere near her. She began to shiver with fear and with the damp night chill that settled over the earth.

Suddenly, a warm woolen jacket was tossed over her. A soft, masculine whisper touched her ears. "Please, shut up for a while, and we'll dispose of the gag."

She swallowed hard and nodded. Screaming wasn't going to get her anywhere up here anyway.

He untied the gag. She breathed deeply. She felt him watching her in the darkness, waiting for whatever she might try to do. She lay still, then flinched as he moved toward her, but he was only adjusting his jacket over her shoulder.

"Is that any better, ma'am?" he asked.

It was insane, really insane. His voice was so deep and husky. Masculine. A sexy voice.

She was *going* insane. He was a madman, and she was thinking that he had an arresting voice, a sensual one. . . .

"Please, try to understand," he continued. "I really don't want to hurt you. I don't even want to hold you here. I just can't take any chances."

Bewildered and exhausted, Vickie held silent. She felt him lie down beside her, stretching out, just inches away. She closed her eyes tightly. Was he dangerous? How did one deal with such a misguided, demented madman? Humor him? Keep fighting him? Stay still?

She'd always suspected she should have taken more psychology classes in college instead of music and art.

What did they say to do on all those news programs?

Memory eluded her.

He was so close to her. Lying beside her. Warm, human, and masculine. He had to sleep. She would lie still; she would feign exhaustion and pretend to sleep herself. And in the darkness of night, when he was deeply sleeping, she would manage to stumble to her feet and slip away.

Vickie shrieked anew at his sudden motion in the night. "Sorry," he apologized abruptly, but he wasn't sorry enough to keep from tethering her bound wrists to one of his own with another long strip of her skirt. She heard it ripping, felt it pulled taut. Terror filled her again.

Now. Surely, he was determined on rape or something worse. . . .

But he was not. He lay down beside her again. She felt his warmth again. Heard his breathing in the night.

She stared numbly at the velvet sky. Night had come in earnest. Ironically, it was beautiful. The night heavens were a deep, black velvet color, touched by a thousand tiny stars that seemed to dazzle in a sea of tranquillity. The moon had risen now and sat high above her, casting a gentle, golden light down upon them.

Then suddenly, a cloud came creeping slowly over the moon. Inch by inch, it stole away the gentle light. From somewhere, she heard the high, mournful cry of a wolf.

It couldn't be a wolf, it couldn't be. They hadn't had wolves in this area in years and years....

There it went again. Distant, dim. The night seemed to have grown very cold. Tremors seemed to dance down her spine. She shivered, feeling as if someone had walked over her grave.

What was she doing to herself? She knew this mountain, loved it...

And she was suddenly terrified of it! Shivering, watching a dark cloud, listening to the howl of the wind or...

Something.

He lay closer to her. She blinked back sudden tears, amazed to be grateful that he was near her. Yes, he was her kidnapper, but he was strong and solid against the dark clouds in the night....

It was his fault that she was here!

But it didn't matter. She inched closer to him. And oddly, he was the protection against the fear she couldn't grasp or see.

She should fear him! she warned herself.

And she stared up at the dark sky, teeth clenched tightly together as she wondered whether to pray for the break of day...

Or pray instead that the night might last forever.

CHAPTER TWO

She was shivering. Somewhere deep in the night, she had been dreaming about being kidnapped, about being tied up, and now she was cold and shivering. Her nightmare, however, was very deep, and she couldn't seem to wake from it. She kept shivering.

Then suddenly, she was warm. Something was around her shoulders, comforting her against the cold. She was held close, tenderly, and felt the sun-sweet warmth entering into her body, into the length of her. The dreams faded, then disappeared. She was wrapped in a curious fog of security and she slept very well.

Then she awoke. Slowly. She heard birds chirping. Light seemed to beat against her eyelids. She felt the tickle of dew-damp grass against her nose.

She opened her eyes. Slowly.

And she saw the mountain, saw the grass. And the sky. Very beautiful today. Blue, with just a few wisps of soft white clouds. Extraordinary. They seemed to sweep by at a very swift speed, gentle, intangible.

Her nose itched. She wanted to scratch it. She couldn't move her arms. They were cramped and stiff.

But she was still warm. Despite the mountain, despite the chill of night that the sun had yet to burn away.

And she realized with a strangled little gasp of fear that her nightmares had been the truth, and any sense of comfort had been the greatest lie. She had been kidnapped. She was still being held. No one had come to rescue her in the night.

And her false sense of security had come from the very man who had caused this horror. His wool cavalry jacket was over her shoulders, and since she had probably shivered through that anyway, he had used the length and curve of his own body against hers to give her warmth. And his arm had come around her, and he held her still.

She almost cried out loud, but choked back the sound. What could she do? Could she possibly escape him in any way now? Ease from his hold, work upon the bonds that he had created from her own skirt hem?

First, she had to rid herself of him! She clenched her teeth together hard, trying to shift out of the draping cover of his arm. She shimmied and inched until she was free from his weight and his touch, and a great sense of relief came sweeping over her. She could manage this.

She tried to lie still and work studiously with her wrists, desperate to ease them from the fabric, equally desperate to keep still. She managed to undo the strip of fabric that tied her to her abductor. But her wrists were still bound up tight. Determined, she kept up the effort, feeling the tiny little beads of sweat break out on her brow, even though it was still very early morning, and the sun had yet to make the day warm at all.

Ease it, ease it . . .

She worked forever, feeling the sun, listening to the birds. She was almost free, could almost taste the sweetness of freedom. And then she heard him, heard his slow deep drawl, his words laced with a certain amusement.

"Ma'am, just what *do* you think you're doing?"

She flung over on her back, staring at him, longing to strike him with all her strength. He was up on an elbow, completely relaxed, watching her efforts with grave humor. He had been awake all along, she was certain. He had been watching her all the while she had been struggling to free her wrists. There was a subtle curve to his lips, a striking light to his silver-gray eyes. For a moment, despite her renewed fury and fear, she was taken aback again by his appearance. Morning's light did all manner of good things for him. Despite the shadowed hint of stubble on his cheeks, the lines and planes of his face were even more arresting, clean, almost *noble!* The curve of his mouth was hauntingly sensual, the flash of his eyes and the tousled length of his hair were startlingly appealing.

This was the man who had kidnapped her.

Her wrists weren't quite free. Her feet were. She lashed out with them strongly, furiously, catching his shins with a vengeance. "You sly, mealymouthed—"

"Eh!" His interruption was swift and frightening. Her feet had landed hard against his legs, and now he was landing hard against her. With swift agility he pounced, straddling over her waist, her bound wrists caught in either of his hands. She gritted her teeth, wildly trying to roll and free herself again, and managing to go nowhere. "Stop it!" he commanded.

She went still, staring up at him. "This has gone too far!" she cried out, trying very hard to remain calm. "It has gone too far! Let me go!"

He shook his head slowly, and seemed unhappy, weary suddenly. So weary, and so very worn, that for a startling moment, she wanted to reach out and touch his cheek.

"I'm sorry," he told her. "I cannot."

"What are you going to do with me?" she demanded, losing her breath in the effort.

"Well, you know," he said very softly, "I've been trying to assure you that I don't intend you any harm. But I've got to find a doctor. And I've got to get back to John. And I can't be taken right now. I can't be. You've got to understand. It's a matter of life and death."

She shook her head, feeling the prick of tears behind her eyelids. "It's not real!"

One tawny brow flew up. He sat back on his haunches, still straddling over her but keeping his weight on his own legs, rubbing his stubbled chin as he looked down at her. "Not real?" he repeated. "Well, hel—" he began, but broke off abruptly. "Not real, hmm? None of us ever thought it was going to be real. Not like this. Not the Yanks, not the Rebs. We each thought we could beat the other in a matter of weeks. Fooled ourselves, all of us. But it's real. And it's John who is dying somewhere, and I've got to go back. And you're going to help me. You're obviously in deep with the Yanks around here. I need to know their positions, and you're going to give them to me."

She inhaled sharply. He wanted to know their positions? Well, they were posted all over town!

"That's it? You want to know where the Yanks are," she asked carefully, "and then you'll let me go?"

She saw his jaw twist slightly. "I may need you with me for a while."

"Oh!" she exclaimed, feeling a fresh wave of fury sweep through her. "Damn you, you've got to let me up! My grandfather is going to be worried sick. People are going to be looking for me. They'll string you up like smoked bacon if you don't let me go and let me go *now!*"

"I'm sure that lots of people are looking for me," he replied wearily. "They always are. But I'm not going to rot in any Yankee prison camp. Not now. So pay attention to me, and pay attention good. *I do not want to hurt you!* But the more you cross me, well, the more you're going to suffer, I'm afraid."

"You're insane!" she cried out. "The Yanks aren't going to arrest you and put you in any prison camp! They've already won the damned war! They've—"

"What?"

Incredulous, he was leaning down, staring at her. She felt the tension and the fevered heat in his body and she was both suddenly very afraid and, at the same time, remarkably aware of him as a man.

Dear God. He was insane. She had to be insane, too. No, she had just been alone way too long. It had been so long since Brad had been killed, and he had been too wonderful when he had lived. She'd simply missed him too much, and so she was finding this lunatic sensual and oddly arresting.

"The Yanks have won the war!" she spat out.

"They haven't!" he cried out furiously, silver eyes flashing now. "I'd have known if it had been that bad!

Stonewall would have never just turned all in, surrendered. I know damned well that the Yanks haven't won yet!''

"Fine!" she shrieked. "And it's just fine, too! They will put you in jail when they get their hands on you! They'll stuff you in a cell, and they'll throw away the key. It will be a nicely padded cell, and—"

She broke off suddenly because he had pulled away, instantly alert and aware, listening.

Someone was coming! she thought suddenly.

"Help!" she cried out. "Hel—"

His hand fell flat over her mouth, so firmly that she couldn't muffle out another sound. She stared at him with daggers in her eyes; she tried to bite. He ignored her, staring toward a clump of bushes.

A jackrabbit suddenly bounded out. It stared at them for a moment, its nose moving a million miles a minute in terror, then it leapt on by.

Great. She was screaming for help—from a rabbit.

His hand fell away. He sat back with a sigh of relief, but eyed her with a deep weariness and warning in his gaze. "For your sake, for my sake, behave."

"Behave! You've taken me as a prisoner! Prisoners do not *behave!* You must be—"

"Thirsty. Very thirsty. And the first thing that you're going to do for me is find a stream. I know we were camped on one for a while, but I seem to have lost my bearings."

She studied him, wishing suddenly and desperately that he wasn't a madman.

"I'll get you to a stream," she told him.

"A stream without Yanks!" he warned.

She lifted her hands toward him, silently imploring that he untie her.

He hesitated. She felt as if fingers closed around her heart. Dear God, it *seemed* real. It seemed so very, very real to him. He didn't want to hurt her. He was just a desperate man. . . .

The war had been over now for more than a hundred and twenty-five years. It couldn't be real. He had to be a madman. Or a paid actor, and that would even be worse.

Yet, to her surprise, he untied her wrists, staring into her eyes all the while. "Don't make me hurt you. Please. Don't try to escape me. My situation is desperate, and I need your help. And if you try to cross me again . . ."

His voice trailed away. She felt a curious trembling, deep within.

"Then what?" she demanded.

"I'll have to remember that you're the enemy."

"What makes you think that I'm the enemy? I was born here, on this mountain," she said quickly.

He smiled again. A slow, wry smile. "Well, ma'am, you were mighty tight with the Yanks down there. And that usually only happens if you're on their side. Or making real good money from them."

To her amazement, that one took a moment to sink in to her. And the moment it hit was the moment that her hands were freed. She struck out at him wildly, heedless at that moment that he might be a madman. "How dare you, how dare you! How dare you make any such implication about me! You—"

"Whoa!" He had caught her wrists again. But she was really furious and twisting and wriggling with a burst of pent-up tension and they did go rolling, picking up speed as they flipped over and over one another in a rapid descent down the mountain. She cried out, suddenly frightened by the force that had seized them. She felt his hand cupping her head then, and his arm encircling her. His body was taking the brunt of their long fall, and he was doing his damnedest to protect her from danger and damage.

They rolled to a halt at last. For a moment they were both dead still. Vickie could hear his heavy breathing, and feel the length of him, his hand still cradling her skull, the bulk of his tightly muscled body very hard and vital against hers. She felt herself trembling, and close to tears. And there was a curious voice whispering in the back of her mind.... Why did he have to be crazy? Why couldn't he be someone sane, whom she'd met in the usual, sane way?

"Are you all right?"

She nodded jerkily, desperate for him to free her, to not touch her so... closely.

"I'll get you to the stream—" she began, but then she slammed her hands against his shoulders, pushing him from her, her own eyes flashing. "But no more! I don't know if you're a mental case, or if someone is paying you to do this to me, but if you make one more insinuation about me, I'll rot and die with you before I'll make a move, do you understand?"

He didn't answer right away. He stood up, and reached down, offering her his hand. She didn't take it. Her eyes narrowed. "Do you understand?"

He caught her hand, pulled her to her feet without her consent. She stood very close to him and he did not release her. "Then what were you doing with the Yanks?" he demanded softly. "You've got to be a whore or a spy," he said huskily.

He caught her wrist when she would have slapped him. "All right, I'm sorry!" he said, and she found herself drawn against him, as he held tightly to the hand with which she had tried to slap him. "I'm sorry, I'm sorry. But you still haven't answered my question."

"I went to see friends!" she cried out passionately.

Something in the truth of her words seemed to touch him. He was still for a long moment, then said softly, "Well, I can understand that. Seems like I meet a lot of my old friends at the end of a sword."

She lowered her eyes quickly. When he spoke, it was just the same. It was with such ardor, such emotion. He was mad, she thought. He had to be.

"I'll take you to the stream," she told him.

"And not to the Yanks?"

"And not to anyone, not now," she said. She turned, and started back up the way that they had come. The most beautiful little spring meandered alongside the little valley just on the other side of the slope. She had always loved to ride alongside it.

Her heart started to pound. Maybe someone would be there. Someone who knew that she was missing.

And then again, she thought woefully, maybe nobody even knew she was missing as yet! Maybe Gramps would think that she had stayed at the encampment. He would keep shaking his head—just like this madman—wondering how she could spend the night with the enemy. But he might not be worried. Unless Arabesque had returned home without her. But

Arabesque might not have made it home. She might have been waylaid by one of the cavalrymen on either side, and the reenactors might be running around, trying to find out who the horse belonged to. And they wouldn't be worried about her at the encampment, because they would be certain that she, who knew the area like the back of her hand, would have made it home, safe and sound.

She swallowed hard, aware that he was following behind her.

Just over the crest of the mountain, she saw the deep valley below. She saw the silver trickle of the stream, and the deep lush field of forest and trees that sloped away on either side.

The Yanks were encamped far down to her left.

The Rebels were encamped way down to her right. Neither of the encampments was visible because of the dense forest of trees. In fact, no one was visible at all from here. No houses, no barns. Just forests and trees and cornfields.

She didn't look back. She kept walking, hurrying for the water. She was all right, she told herself. She was convinced that he didn't intend to hurt her. So what did that mean? He was insane, obviously insane. But he wasn't dangerous. So she just had to humor him. Humor him, and keep him at his distance....

He had stopped behind her, she realized. She paused herself and looked back. He was staring over the mountaintop, seeing the view. She felt a little tremor in her heart again. He was enjoying it. Tremendously. His eyes touched hers, deeply silver.

"It's very beautiful," he said softly. "And peaceful. Like Eden." His eyes left hers, running over the exquisite scenery once again. "It's amazing, isn't it? From here, you might think that we were alone in all the world. And even in summer, the colors are so radiant. Purple and green and blue, and all touched by the yellow of those wild daisies over there. You'd never know that there was war," he said, and voice was very husky, barely a breath. "Never. In a thousand years. It's like the most beautiful place on earth."

"It is the most beautiful place on earth," she heard herself reply softly. Then she was oddly embarrassed, and she turned and hurried downward now, anxious to reach the little stream that was fed from the fresh springs deep within the earth.

He followed her again, staying close. He had given her a certain freedom now. But she realized that if she were to make the slightest move, he could pounce on her in a second. He didn't trust her.

They were certainly even on that score.

She paused at the streambed, kneeling down. She was amazingly thirsty. It had been a long night. Heedless of him for a moment, she cupped her hands in the cool water and brought them to her lips and drank deeply.

He had gone a step farther, striding right into it, burying his face in it. He soaked his throat and his sleeves and half his shirt. Vickie sat back, watching him. Then she ripped off more of her hem, wet it and dripped the cool water around her throat and neck, lifting her hair, relishing the sweet feel of it. She closed her eyes, listening to the movement of the water and feeling the sun. Then she opened her eyes, and discovered him staring at her, and the expression in his silver eyes was a startling one, a *hungry* one.

But it was quickly gone. He blinked, and once again his gaze and expression revealed nothing to her—nothing except hardness and determination. She stood quickly, aware then that she had done a good job of soaking herself. Her calico day dress was glued to her breasts.

"What now?" he asked a little bit desperately.

She was startled when he suddenly walked over to her. He lifted her left hand. His eyes were like blades on hers as his fingers moved over the simple gold wedding band there.

"Husband?" he asked her.

She felt a rise of color flood to her cheeks. She wrenched her hand free. "Dead," she lashed out.

"The war?"

"Yes." Then she realized that he meant *this* war. "He was killed in Iraq," she said swiftly. And despite herself, she heard bitter words fall from her lips. *"Friendly fire."*

"His own artillery?" he demanded.

Her eyes widened. At least he understood that. She nodded.

"Iraq?" he queried.

She sighed. Oh, he was good. There hadn't been any such place known as *Iraq* during the Civil War. Or the War Between the States, as Gramps was determined to call it.

"Never mind," she said wearily.

"Which army was he fighting for?" he demanded.

With a groan, Vickie sank down on the damp stream embankment. She shook her head. "We just have one army now. Just one."

He knelt down before her. He touched her chin, lifting it so that he could see into her eyes. "Which army?"

"The United States Army," she said wearily. "You don't believe me." She shook her head again, trying desperately to understand how this attractive, masculine and appealing man could be a maniac. "You must be a business exec who has snapped," she said flatly. "Hey, I understand, the pressure today can do it. People do just snap."

"I haven't snapped," he said angrily. "And I don't believe you! We haven't surrendered. We fight better. It's our homeland. And Stonewall wouldn't surrender us."

"Stonewall is dead," she said flatly.

He wrenched her up suddenly by her shoulders. "What?" he demanded fiercely.

"Stonewall Jackson is dead. But then again, so is Lincoln. Lee is dead, Grant is dead! Heck, Jefferson Davis survived them all, but damn it, he's dead now, too!"

"Stop it! I don't believe you, I don't believe any of it—"

"We're in the midst of the 1990s—"

"It's 1862—"

"No, no! You're all pretending that it's 1862! Please, get a grip on it all!" Vickie pleaded. "I'm telling you that it's—"

"And I'm telling you to stop it! Stop it now!" he cried angrily, rising. "It's 1862. This battle is still going and I've got to find my brother! He's hurt, he's injured and he's going to die—"

"No one will let him die!" Vickie cried. "There are emergency vehicles all over—"

"If the Yanks take him, he will die!" he cried passionately, silver eyes raking her once again.

To her amazement, she felt tears stinging her eyes once again. Mad or not, he believed it. He believed every word that he was saying to her.

"I don't know how to convince you!" she whispered miserably. "No one will hurt your brother. They'll help him, I swear it."

He was silent for a moment, then he turned away. "I wish that I could believe you," he told her.

His hands were on his hips. Vickie saw a glint there. She didn't know why, but she was standing suddenly. She strode through the shallow water to where he was standing, heedless of her boots. She reached for his left hand. There was a plain gold band there, too.

"Wife?" she queried, feeling as if she had choked on the word just a little bit.

She felt him go tense, swallowing hard. "Dead," he said huskily. And he added quickly, "And I don't know where the fire came from, a Yank gun or a Rebel gun. We had a home out on the peninsula. An old place," he added in a rush. "Built before 1700." He turned around, squinting as he stared up the mountain. "Well, it's burned to the ground now. And my wife is buried nearby." His eyes touched upon Vickie's. "It isn't very friendly fire, is it?"

She shook her head. Then she realized that she was agreeing with this man. He had told her that his wife had been killed by stray fire in the middle of a battle, a *Civil War* battle, and she was agreeing that it was possible.

She hurried over to him suddenly. "Listen to me, please listen to me. You've got to understand. You need help—"

"Oh, indeed! I need help, lots of it."

"You believe all this, don't you?" she whispered.

He was reaching into his pocket, pulling out something square and whitish. He broke it with a hard snap, offering her half. Hardtack. She'd seen the stuff in museums all her life, and Gramps even had a few scraps of it in his prized collection of Civil War memorabilia.

This was so very real....

Reenactors made it, she reminded herself. Just like they made clothing, and guns and swords. Just like they pitched tents, and sang songs.

"It's not much, but it's all I've got," he told her. He walked over to stand by one of the trees, looking out over the valley. He took a crunchy bite out of his hardtack. Vickie looked down at the chunk of supposedly digestible food she held. Her stomach rumbled. She was starving. She hadn't eaten much last night.

"Eat this...?" she murmured. But just then, she thought that she saw something very tiny within it moving. Something the same whitish color. Something like a...

A weevil. A creature. A maggot. She didn't know what. Something completely horrible.

She shrieked and threw the piece of food high into the air, backing away from it.

Instantly he was at her side, taking her into his arms, and looking anxiously about. "What, what is it? Where?" He held her close, protectively, against him, drawing a gun from the holster at his side. It was a repeater, Vickie realized. She didn't know guns that well, but she thought that it was one of the Colt repeating rifles. It was large by current-day standards for a handgun....

But then, once again, she'd seen the like in Gramps's precious glass-encased collection shelves before.

He stared at her hand. "What happened? Is there a snake? Have you been bitten? What is it?"

She shook her head wildly, staring at him. "A *thing*, a white thing. In that piece of food you gave me. It moved."

Now he was looking at her as if she were the one who had gone absolutely mad.

"What?"

She shook her head, feeling sick.

He walked across the grass and found the piece of hardtack. He stared at it, then turned to look at her, troubled.

"This is pretty good," he said, studying her with a puzzled frown. "Why, there's only a maggot or two in it."

"A maggot—or *two?*" she whispered. "Oh!" she said, turning around, clutching her stomach.

She closed her eyes tightly. His hands were on her shoulders and he spun her around. "I'm sorry!" he said gruffly. "It's all I've got. I'll catch you something later. But for the moment—"

She shook her head violently. "I'm not hungry anymore."

"I've got to find my troops," he told her softly.

A breeze stirred. His hands were still on her shoulders; he seemed incredibly tall, broad shouldered, strikingly handsome. His silver eyes were passionate, the lean hard planes of his face and the square of his jaw all spoke of determination and a curious valor. "I've got to find the Yanks, and I've got to find my own troops."

"And you've got to have me to do it?" she whispered.

He nodded gravely.

"I can't let you go. You have to see that."

"I wish you'd believe me," she said. She wished she could help him snap out of his delusion. She wished he would suddenly be quite normal and they could start all over again. She wished . . .

What *was* she thinking?'

"Come on," he said softly, "let's go." But his hands were still on her shoulders. And suddenly he brushed her cheek with his knuckles. The motion was infinitely tender, and she closed her eyes for a moment, savoring it.

Then she swallowed hard, pulling away from him, her eyes lowered.

Even if he wasn't a *complete* lunatic, he certainly wasn't all there. And he'd already accused her of enough things!

Her eyes raised to his, and she was ready with a quick retort. It died in her throat. There was that desperate emotion in his eyes! Pain, determination . . . tenderness. She shook her head, with no voice to speak.

"I don't even know your name," he told her huskily.

"Victoria," she murmured softly. "Vickie."

"Jason," he murmured.

"Not colonel?" she inquired.

"Only if you intend to follow orders," he said with a curious, almost wistful smile.

"Well, I don't follow orders," she informed him.

"Then," he said, bowing formally, "I suppose I'll have to ask you politely to help me find the enemy troops—and my own."

"And if I refuse?" she said.

"Then I'll have to order you around," he said, catching her arm. "It's time to move on," he insisted, "Victoria."

Her name was soft coming from his lips. So soft.

His hand on her arm was absolutely insistent.

And once again, they were moving over the mountain.

CHAPTER THREE

Vickie had always thought that she knew the mountain better than the back of her own hand; however, that day, she seemed to lose her own bearings, too.

Gramps's house should have been to the west and the encampments should have been down in the valley to her extreme south. When she walked toward what she thought should have been the Rebel encampments, she realized that she had led him down a trail that was way too far north.

And walking on these slopes and inclines was much harder than riding over them. She had led him around in silence for hours, it seemed, when she realized her mistake. And then, of course, he stared at her as if she had done it all on purpose, and was trying to get him captured or cause something even worse to happen to him.

The strangest thing about the afternoon was that she was beginning to believe him. What he was saying couldn't possibly be true, and yet he was incredibly sincere and passionate and he just . . .

He acted so different. He looked different. He talked different. He was different. From anyone she knew. And no matter how she fought against it, there was something so compelling because of those differences.

His hand suddenly fell upon her shoulder. He pulled her to a halt. She whirled around and looked at him. A trickle of sweat slipped down the handsome planes of his face. A deep sandy brow arched to her and those hard silver-gray eyes of his seemed to fix her where she stood.

"Where are you taking me?" he asked her.

She lifted her hands and shook her head, "I'm trying. I swear it, I'm trying."

"To get me where?"

"To the Rebel encampment."

A cloud fell over his eyes. One of suspicion. "Hmm. So it seems."

"Damn you! Damn you!" she cried to him suddenly, slamming her fists against his chest and actually pushing him back with her force. Taken by surprise, he caught her wrists, and she was pulled up flush against his body again, held there while their hearts hammered together, her head cast back, throat arched, eyes blazing into his. No matter how he held her, she was determined to speak. "I'm just dying to get you to the Rebel encampment—sir! I'm dying for someone else to tell you that you're a madman, that this war has been over—I'm dying for you to believe me!"

Something in his hold seemed to ease. Yet he didn't release her. But the way that he stared at her changed. And the way that he held her changed, too.

"And I'm dying for you to believe me," he said very softly.

She relaxed in his hold. There was a trembling beginning deep within her. Truly, she was the one not in her right senses. When he held her, she wanted him to continue to do so. She wanted to rest her head against his shoulder, test the texture of his cavalry shirt. She wanted his hands to fall upon the length of her hair and soothe her.

And then...

Then she wanted more.

She felt her cheeks begin to burn as she tried to keep her stare level with his. This was really madness. She knew so many nice young men. All the fine young fellows Gramps kept bringing around so persistently. Friends. Friends of friends. All of them so usual, normal—and sane.

But since she had lost her husband, she hadn't felt the first spark of desire....

Until now. Until she had come upon this silver-eyed madman. Now she was feeling a surge of responses she had thought long buried, along with a handsome young man in a very different soldier's uniform.

She opened her mouth to speak, trying to shake the startling sensation of warmth that had filled her. No words came at first. She struggled. "I—I must believe you in a way," she said. "I believe that you believe what you're saying, anyway." She spun around quickly, eyes suddenly, inexplicably, filled with tears. "Come on. I'll get us somewhere, I promise."

She had barely begun walking when the day seemed to darken. She looked up. The morning had been beautiful. It had suddenly turned gray. Dark, billowing clouds raced across the sky. She had never seen clouds move so rapidly before. They made her uneasy. Just like that strange cry in the night had made her uneasy. She gritted her teeth, fighting the strange—and ridiculous—sensation of fear.

"We're in for some weather," she cried. What was the matter with her? She felt so cold. The world seemed so strange. As if she was treading where she shouldn't be treading, walking through a graveyard at midnight. She had a strange intuition, telling her she'd crossed some forbidden line. She was seeing things she wasn't meant to see. But again, she tried to assure herself that she was being ridiculous.

But Jason, too, had been looking up at the wild, darkening sky. His eyes touched hers. There was a strange expression in them, as if he had seen this strange "weather" before, as if he, too, had felt cold slivers of ice in the pit of his stomach. But he nodded to her, a smile of reassurance quickly curving his lips as he read her expression.

"There are a few caves near here. Let's get to one!" she said.

He reached for her hand. Just as they touched, a tremendous bolt of lightning flashed down near them, so blindingly visible that it was like watching ancient Zeus cast down a jagged streak of fire. The thunder that rolled and clashed in its wake was instant and alarming.

Vickie looked up. The sky was nearly black. It had happened in a matter of minutes.

"Jason!"

"Come closer!"

His arm was around her, as if he could combat invisible dragons, yet she was delighted to be with him, glad of his arm, of the comfort and the security.

Oddly, against the tempest of the sky, the rain that started then was light. Almost a mist. Of course, it could be just heralding the real storm to come. Right now, it was soft, cool. Like the breeze, it seemed to wrap around her with invisible threads, a spider's web to hold and haunt her. Despite the softness of the rain, the look of the day was still wicked, the black sky churning and spinning.

"Let's go!" It was Jason who started moving.

The wind began to whip anew. Vickie realized that in the sudden darkness, they were running blindly once again. She didn't know where they were going.

The caves were . . . to their left?

"This way!" she cried out suddenly, certain of her own direction. But was she? The trees were dipping and swaying, bowed down beneath the strength of the wind. They seemed to form a maze in the darkness.

The two ran through the lashing trees. A field of electricity snapped and crackled around them. It seemed that they ran forever, and then they burst into a clearing.

She could see. The wind still lashed at them, the day seemed stranger than ever. The sky roiled. But the blackness had somewhat abated, and she could see before her. Horsemen were coming. Relief filled her. Men were practicing for the reenactment battles still to come. They were riding toward her and Jason now. All she had to do was cry out and wave to them. They would get her home. She would bring Jason. Introduce him to Gramps, and Gramps would know what to do. All that she had to do was cry out, and she could get home. The danger had passed.

She slammed to a stop with Jason right behind her. She felt his fingers on her shoulders, digging in.

"Jason! They'll help us—" she began.

"Help us, my foot!" he cried. "Look at the uniform!"

Yankee. She tried to explain. "Jason, they're reenactors. They're not going to—"

She heard an explosion, then felt the heat as something whistled by her cheek. There was a flat, slamming sound behind her. She swirled around, white and stunned.

She could see where the bullet intended for her had embedded into a tree.

The men in the mist were really shooting at them. Real Civil War soldiers, shooting real bullets. . . .

It couldn't be! Only ghosts could travel these mountains—ghosts and memories—and neither could shoot real guns. Perhaps they were reenactors after all, intent on murder.

Dully, she thought, no. No motive. Men didn't go crazy all in a group.

A second whistle caressed her cheek. Another bullet whizzed by, just missing her.

"Get behind me!"

"But they're not real—"

"The hell they're not!"

She was behind him, shoved there, with the bulk of his body protecting her.

"They wouldn't be shooting at me—" she protested weakly.

"They can't see a damn thing in this rain and mist!" he assured her. "They don't mean to be shooting at a woman. You're standing in the middle of their battle."

One of them suddenly broke from the pack and came riding down upon them. She heard the rip of the steel as Jason pulled his cavalry sword from his scabbard. The thunderous sound of the horse's hooves came bearing down upon them hard. She barely saw the man upon the horse. She did see the muted glint of his sword, raised and ready to strike. She cried out.

Jason deflected the blow that was coming their way with a hideous clash of steel. His return was so forceful that the horseman wavered on his mount and then came crashing down to the ground. He started to struggle to his feet.

"Get back!" Jason commanded Vickie. Stunned, disbelieving, she did so, backing away just a few feet. The breeze that touched her cheeks now seemed very cold indeed. She stared, numb, stunned, as the Yankee stood and approached Jason, his sword waving. He was young, a teenager.

She still couldn't believe what was happening right before her eyes. She couldn't believe that Jason and this boy were fighting with swords, that they would bleed, that one of them would kill the other, right in front of her, here and now....

It couldn't be real.

She had lost her own mind.

The boy approached. But Jason was good. His sword rose and fell, striking the boy's. The sword went flying.

"Oh, God, don't hurt him!" Vickie cried out.

Jason looked to her quickly. She could hear the pounding of horses' hooves again. Other Yankees were about to bear down on them.

He turned around and caught the young soldier with a good blow to his cheek. He fell quickly, but there were at least five or six horses pounding toward them now. A bullet flew. This one nearly caught Vickie in the arm. Startled, she cried out. His body was suddenly shoved up in front of hers again, protecting her from whatever might come. "Let's go. Get your head down!"

They started to run, back through the arbor. They ran until Vickie suddenly caught her foot on a tree root. She fell hard, dragging Jason down with her. And they were suddenly rolling again. Hard, slamming against the earth. And it seemed that they rolled and rolled forever until they came to a stopgap of a valley.

The sky above them was still black. The misty rain was still falling.

But the sound of battle was gone. Completely. Jason lay on top of Vickie, staring down at her. She looked up at him incredulously.

He smiled suddenly. "At least you're not a known spy."

"What?"

"If those Yanks hadn't fired at you, I would have been extremely worried."

What kind of a nightmare had she entered? Had she imagined what had happened, or had it been real? It had all happened so very, very fast. And now the soldiers were gone. All gone. There were just the two of them on the mountain again, staring at one another in a very fine mist of rain.

"They couldn't have been real," she said dully. "They were just reenactors, getting carried away." But things had been so real! She could remember that awful thunking sound of the bullet embedding in the tree.

She could remember the feel of it, whizzing by her face, the hot metal so very nearly touching her. . . .

She could also remember the way that the cold breeze had touched her. The deep, almost primal fear that had filled her when they had come to that strange place. She couldn't shake the feeling that she had walked into some forbidden place, that she had stumbled into some other dimension.

All that had kept her sane then, kept her from shrieking out, had been Jason—Jason's touch. . . .

But Jason couldn't be sane.

Oh, God! She closed her eyes quickly, opened them again. It was over. The strange clouds were gone. The feelings of fear were gone. And he was eyeing her very speculatively again.

"You did bring me to the Yanks," he said thoughtfully, staring at her.

"You son of a—" she began, but cut off suddenly. He wouldn't be accustomed to such language. Young women of any breeding back then watched their tongues carefully. What would he think?

What was she thinking? "You son of a bi—sea serpent!" she strangled out. "This whole thing is insane, the world is insane and it all started since I had the ill fortune to wander into you! I wasn't—"

Another bolt of lightning flashed wildly in the sky, interrupting her tirade. Thunder cracked loudly in its wake.

"It's really going to rain now," he said brusquely. He leapt agilely to his feet and pulled her up to him. He seemed to hold her for a brief moment, weighing his options. Again, she felt absurdly protected, secure, content and somehow right in his arms.

No...

Vickie shivered. Everyone was gone indeed. Had the soldiers been reenactors? Had she imagined the whiz of the bullets?

Maybe Jason wasn't even real....

But he was. His fingers curled warmly around hers.

"The caves," she whispered. "We need to get to the caves."

"I think that I'll lead this time," he said softly, and proceeded to do so. He turned about and stared around for a moment, then started off. Lightning lit up the entire sky for an instant. The thunder that followed caused Vickie to jump. The rain was starting to come harder. He slipped his arm around her shoulders, and hurried onward.

She didn't watch where they were going. And she didn't know how he managed to find the caves, but he did. Leading in a southeasterly course downhill, he brought them to the few small caves she had known since she was a child. They came upon them just as the rain really started, bursting down suddenly as if floodgates had been opened. Vickie stood just inside the entryway, shivering. Jason stood just behind her.

A second later, lightning flared again. Vickie let out a startled scream, for it struck so close that it hit one of the tall trees just across from the entrance to the cave. She watched with fascination as sparks flew from the tree.

Then it began to fall. Toward her.

"Jesu, Mary and Joseph!" Jason swore suddenly. Before she knew it, he was on top of her, the force of his body carrying them both down to the floor of the cave—and away from the heavy trunk section of tree that came slamming down where Vickie had been standing just seconds before.

She looked from the tree trunk to the man who now lay atop her once again. Her breath caught and she trembled suddenly. Who was he?

Did it matter?

He had taken her captive, yes.

He might well be a madman on a mountain.

But time and time again, he had protected her. He had set himself between her and any threat of danger. For so long, she had barely felt alive.

And when he touched her...

She wanted to live again. And feel again. Everything.

He didn't move. Not for the longest time. Silver-gray eyes touched hers, searching for something, seeing something.... She wasn't sure what.

Then his hand moved, just slightly, the knuckle of his forefinger moving gently over her cheek. She felt that sensual stroke as if it enveloped the length of her with a curious warmth and magic.

Then she watched with fascination as he slowly lowered his head, and touched her lips with his own.

She didn't protest. She couldn't have done so had she wanted to. Sheer fascination held her still, let her feel the surging warmth and slow demand of that touch. His mouth formed over hers, the masculine scent of him seemed to fill her senses, the vital strength and tension of his body seemed to encompass hers in the most arousing way. It had been so long. She shouldn't be doing this, shouldn't be feeling this. Her heart had lain dormant so very long....

This stirring wasn't her heart, she told herself.

But in a way, it was. For his manner, his eyes, his ways, all had touched her as surely as the lips that now formed around her own.

His mouth on hers had been warm; it was suddenly hot. It had been forming and molding and coercive....

Now it was demanding.

Searing with wet heat, the tip of his tongue explored the outline of her lips. Then pressed between them. Deep. Deeper. Moving, exploring, demanding.

Remember, remember the past...a voice whispered deep inside of her.

But she could suddenly let the past slip away. The sweetness, and the pain. The memories of the laughter and the love. She could not conjure up the picture of the face that had once been hers....

The present was upon her. The present, and a man with silver-gray eyes and a will of steel and the most cavalier way of protecting her from harm.

His tongue moved more deeply into her mouth. Stroked in a way that seemed to evoke every fire within her. The rain beat down around them. The floor of the cave was rough and hard. She wasn't aware of any of it, only of the feel of him, the hot rugged hardness of his body, the feel of his mouth upon hers. His tongue. Stroking now in a way that was suggestive of a thousand things to come....

His mouth lifted slowly from hers. His eyes touched down upon hers once again. She stared at him in return, waiting.

His eyes never left hers. In a sudden frenzy, he began undoing the buttons of his cavalry shirt. In seconds it was stripped from his body, and he was balling it into a pillow that he set beneath her head. Her gaze slipped to his chest and it seemed that her heart began to beat harder. It was a nice chest. An incredibly nice chest. He had appeared tall and slim; he was walled with muscle, very broad shouldered, the breadth of him handsomely covered with crisp, sandy blond hair that tapered to a little trail that disappeared enticingly beneath the waistband of his pants.

She dragged her eyes back to his. He watched her still. Waiting for a protest? She didn't know.

But one wasn't coming.

He stood then, and she was watching still. Just as that silver-gray stare of both challenge and determination touched her so continually. Then swept over her. Causing a riot of heat to strike her, causing her to feel the most incredible sensations where he still had yet to touch.

It wasn't real, couldn't be real....

But it was wonderful. Like a strange, exotic dream. The world was filled with the roaring sound of the rain beyond the cave. And beyond that, it was filled with the man. With the muscle-riddled length of him, the warmth of him, the scent of him....

His boots fell on the hard-packed earth of the cave. His socks upon them.

Then he stripped off his cavalry pants. He was authentic to his beliefs, she thought briefly. There were no boxers or B.V.D.s beneath them. He was in long johns.

And they quickly fell upon his socks, and once they did, Vickie couldn't think of the past or the present or anything but the immediate future. Her madman was quite incredible, muscled and bronze from head to toe, trim in the hips with rock-hard thighs.

And boldly, flagrantly aroused. A violent shudder ripped through her at the sight of his raw nakedness. Her eyes shot back to his and she knew that her face was flaming with color.

And oddly, she knew, too, that if she were to protest, even now, the Southern cavalry commander's costume would go back on, piece by piece, long johns to scabbard and boots. But she didn't want to protest. Yet she was still afraid, as if she were about to embark on the wings of an eagle, when she hadn't flown in a long, long time.

He came down on his knees before her. He scooped her into his arms, and her eyes searched out his. Then his lips touched hers once again. Exploded upon them, fierce, demanding, the stroke and length of his tongue a wild pillage within her mouth. Her arms snaked around him, and she held tightly to him, feeling the sweet wildness fill and pervade her. She returned the kiss, fingers winding into the hair at his nape, stroking, caressing. Then he broke away, his eyes touching hers once again. "How can this be ill fortune?" he queried softly, his breath a husky whisper against her cheek.

How indeed?

She shook her head, at a loss for the moment.

"You cannot be real," she assured him.

He arched a brow.

"If you are, then I must surely be a horrible person. A woman who was any kind of lady—"

"Would still feel this!" he swore with a soft but vehement passion.

Maybe. And maybe it was wrong. It didn't matter. She just might wake up and discover that it was all a dream. But until then . . .

Her fingertips cradled his head, drawing him back to her. With a sudden burst of sweet surrender she gave way to all the hunger that had arisen within her, the longing, the fascination. His flesh was hot beneath her fingers, vibrant, so electric with energy and the taut strength of the muscles beneath it. Her fingers inched against his nape, feeling the brush of his hair. She tasted his mouth again, eagerly, parting her lips to his, feeling the sensual roll and thrust of his tongue. And she felt his touch in return, too. The fluid movement of his fingers upon the buttons of her calico day gown. One, and then the next, his knuckles brushing her flesh with each motion, bringing new fire to awaken within her, new aches of longing, yearning to be touched. The garment fell away. She was barely aware of its leaving; she was keenly aware of his stroke and brush of his fingers.

Then she gasped raggedly as his lips broke from hers. She was so deeply involved in her sea of sensation that it took her several minutes to realize that he had gone dead still.

Then she realized that his fingers were set upon the fine lace strap of her rather elegant designer bra. And his eyes were open and incredulous. When he moved again, it was to stroke that strap. His eyes did not leave it. He seemed to have forgotten that he was naked, that she was completely disheveled, and that he'd had her at the brink of one of the rarest and most momentous occasions of her life.

She might have been embarrassed. She might have even been hurt enough to be angry and feel like a fool. The emotions did flash through her. But then she realized his absolute amazement and she closed her eyes.

Someone had really fired a gun at her. As if there was a strange time warp on the mountain. And if that was true, then he was just beginning to really believe it himself, seeing at long last something that did not belong to his world.

No, it couldn't be....

But he was still just staring. Her fingers curled around his. He started, and his eyes met hers. "My God," he murmured hoarsely. "What—is this?"

She hesitated. "A new type of corset," she said simply, watching his eyes. A streak of warmth like a bolt of the lightning that continued to light up the sky now and then seemed to course through her. Did she believe him? Could she believe him?

And how could she do anything else when he stared with such amazement as he did now?

His touch became more intimate than before, yet strangely distanced. With a sudden determination he thrust the calico down from her shoulders and his forefinger drew a line over the trim cut of the elegant little undergarment. Where he touched her, she felt as if she burned. She bit her lip, telling herself that he had become interested in the mechanics of clothing much more than he was interested in the woman wearing that clothing. She felt her cheeks redden.

But then his gaze met hers. And he seemed to realize what he had done, and his arms encompassed her, sweeping her back against him again. Her head rested against his naked chest, and he rocked with her, holding her tight.

"What did you say it is?" he whispered huskily.

"The nineties."

"Eighteen?" he said hopefully.

She eased from his hold to look up. She shook her head. "Nineteen-hundred-type nineties," she told him.

"God," he whispered. "Dear God." He shook his head. "It's impossible. It's impossible. And it can't be. We just came from the scene of a skirmish. How...?"

His voice trailed away. He was right, Vickie thought. *The skirmish had been real. The bullets had been real. So just where were they right now? His world, or her own?*

She closed her eyes tightly. Hers. It had to be her world. Had to be.

Once again, lightning tore across the sky. The thunder crack was loud, deafening. She started, and his arms tightened around her. She stared up into his eyes and stroked his cheek with sudden compassion. "I'm sorry," she murmured. "I'm really sorry." He didn't seem to hear her at first. She eased herself to her knees and took his face between both her hands. She touched his lips with her own, hesitantly, brushing them. Touching them once again with just the tip of her tongue, trying to bring comfort.

But it seemed she brought more. Much more. With that gentle stroke, she stoked the fires already kindling. He encompassed her into his arms, hungrily accepting the kiss, returning it with a fever. He held her for a moment, then began to thrust her unbuttoned dress down farther from her shoulders until she was completely freed from the sleeves and the garment fell unheeded to the dirt flooring beneath them.

He cushioned her fall as he pressed her back to the ground. His fingers were both demanding and tender, brushing her cheek, her throat, her ribs. His lips trailed from hers to press hotly to the pulse that beat so rampantly against her flesh at the hollow base of her collarbone. Then his mouth moved lower, to caress the rise of her breasts above the silk-and-lace confines of the bra.

He looked up at her. A wry smile touched his lips. "How do I free you from this thing?" he asked.

She felt her cheeks flood with color. His smile deepened and he touched her lips briefly with his own. "Never mind, I'll figure it out."

And before she could speak, he had done just that.

Maybe he'd known women who wore a very different kind of undergarment, but apparently, he had found his way around those quite easily.

His fingers had found the center hook of her bra and deftly released it, spilling her breasts free. Then he was still for a second, and she could hear ragged breathing, and she realized that it came from them both and that it mingled on the air.

Then he uttered a hoarse cry, and stretched out beside her, his hands upon her bare flesh, exploring at first, so filled with fascination, with demand, with tenderness. Stroking, cupping, caressing. His palm rotated slowly over her nipple and she felt a little cry escape her own lips. His mouth covered hers. Then left it. Touched her flesh again. At her throat. At the rise of her breasts. Then it covered the fullness of her nipple, the roughened center of his tongue rubbing over and over it. She gasped again, amazed at the surge of desire that swept through her. Liquid fire surged through her limbs, winding into a center where hunger leapt out again like sparks of the liquid blaze.

Her fingers tugged into his hair, streaking over it, through it. She raked her nails gently over the rippled muscles of his shoulders and back, then allowed them to dig in slightly for a moment as a blinding wave of sensation seized her once again. "Please," she whispered, and she had no idea at all what she was asking him for—if she wanted him to move or to stay.

His hand slid low over her abdomen, pushing down the bunched fabric of her dress. He found the long slip she was wearing, yet shoved it easily enough along with the dress, never missing a beat in his lovemaking. His lips trailed down the deep valley between her breasts and farther, touching her hip, her belly. She felt his fingers upon the lace of the sexy panties that matched her bra. And suddenly he was very still.

She squeezed her eyes closed, praying that he wouldn't stop, that he wouldn't force her to think. Then she opened her eyes, and met his gaze. A sweep of fire rose to her cheeks and fanned out through the length of her body in a giant flush.

"You're—" he began, and he shook his head. "You're beautiful," he told her quietly. His eyes swept the length of her, pausing at the bikini panties. Then his hands were on her once again, sweeping her hips toward him. He leaned his face against her belly and her breath caught. He touched her. Drawing imaginary lines over the design in the lace. His knuckles brushed her thighs. His breath was hot against very sensitive flesh. He teased the rim of the panties with the tip of his tongue, and she cried out suddenly, thinking that she couldn't bear such exquisite teasing one second more.

His fingers curled around the band of the panties, and they were suddenly stripped away. And she gasped again with sheer pleasure at the warmth of his body as she felt the fullness of it against her own. His fingers curled into hers, his gaze locked with hers. She felt his hair-roughened legs against her own, felt the angle of his hips, the tantalizing brush of his chest and the fascinating, hot, protruding thrust of his sex. Against her. Against her thighs. Against the acutely sensitive petals of her sex. He held there for a moment, watching her eyes. His right hand released hers and came between them. Brushed her thigh. Touched her. Lightly. More deeply. Entering her. Stoking, Coaxing. Urging her beyond the limits of sensations she'd ever known.

She cried out softly, closing her eyes, burying her face against his shoulder. She felt him shift his weight. His touch was gone. Then it was with her again. She shuddered fiercely as he swept into her with the fullness of himself, seeming to enter her like molten steel, filling every void, touching the very depths of her. Her hands fell upon his back and her fingers dug into his hard muscles. She felt the ripple of muscle as he began to move. Slowly. Just seeming to slip more incredibly deeply into her with each enticing thrust. She would split, she would die, she thought. She did neither. She felt the sweetest rush of fire begin. Bursting from an inner core, streaking like lightning to totally fill her.

Her arms tightened around his back. Her hands moved wildly against him. And in just moments, she felt enveloped in a tempest of unimaginable pleasure, of hunger and magic. Wild streaks of fire, more radiant than lightning, bolted through her again and again. She arched with the wonder of him, writhed to his rhythm.

Aware of the hard earth beneath her, she barely felt it. She knew only the certainty of the force and power of the man, the wild reckless energy that now ruled his desire. He had been so careful at first, so patient and arousing a lover. Yet now he was a hungry one, demanding in each movement, drawing her with him to new heights of magic, receding, lifting her once again. She forgot everything except for the need to rise with him to the sweet blinding pinnacle they both sought. She clung to him, and felt the ragged tension in him as his hands slipped about her hips, holding her tightly as he thrust hard and deeply and held himself within her. A swiftly simmering heat seemed to explode within her, bringing a burst of stars to sweep the streaks of lightning from her world. Diamonds seemed to lay against velvet black. Perhaps she lost touch with this plane of existence for a moment. But she came to, with the hot sweet nectar of release sweeping wildly through her. She felt him moving again, once, shuddering violently, and a greater heat seemed to fill her. Then they were both still.

Slowly, slowly, she felt the earth beneath her once again. Felt the hard ground, the pillow of his cavalry shirt.

Slowly she heard the wild cry of the wind.

Yet it, too, was dying down.

He was damp and slick, lying atop her, then easing his weight from her, but keeping her within the confines of his arms. His fingers moved tenderly over her hair. His lips brushed her forehead.

"Ill fortune," he mused softly. "Yet you are the best thing to happen to me in all these long and bitter months of war."

She moved slightly, amazed now that he could still be there, that he could be holding her. She gritted her teeth, suddenly fighting tears. She wasn't sorry in the least for what she had done. She was amazed once again that he still lay here, that he was not a dream.

Sated now, she took the time to covertly admire her lover, allowing her gaze a leisurely journey over the length of him. There were scars upon his shoulder and back, which she had missed. They caused her to swallow, but they were all that marred his perfection. He was lean, but very well and tightly muscled, his hips so trim, legs so long, thighs so hard.

He lifted her chin suddenly, determined to meet her eyes. She found herself flushing again when she discovered that he was very aware of her scrutiny.

"Isn't it a little late to decide if I pass muster?" he asked lightly.

With a brief smile, she told him that he did. She liked his face even more now, the handsome planes, the gravity in his eyes. She liked the curve of his smile, the tone of his voice. And the tenderness with which he held her now.

"You are wall-to-wall scars," she whispered, her voice trembling. She drew a finger delicately over one of the pale white and jagged lines on his shoulder.

"As I said, it's been a long and bitter war," he murmured.

A long and bitter war....

No. Not this war. This war was just a game. It was history. It was something for Gramps and his cronies to hash over and argue into the wee hours of the night. It couldn't be real.

But to this man, it was.

His thumb and forefinger moved over her cheek. "You are nearly perfection," he said, studying her eyes. "I—"

He broke off suddenly, into a dead silence. His eyes narrowed at her. Then she heard something outside the cave. A rustling that wasn't the wind.

He thrust her from him suddenly and leapt to his feet. Naked and agile. Bronzed muscles flexed and tensed.

"You know where we are, eh?" he roughly demanded.

"What?" she murmured.

"You definitely know how to take a man off guard, Miss Victoria," he drawled in a whisper. His gray eyes, so warm moments ago, were now cold with suspicion.

"Off guard?" she repeated. Then she heard it again. A sound that wasn't the storm, wasn't the wind. Something creeping up to the cave. Furtively.

She leapt up, heedless of her own state of undress. "Of all the nerve!" she whispered back to him, fingers clenching into fists at her side. Then she realized that she was undressed. She snatched up her gown, holding it in front of her. "How dare you! How dare you!"

"Shh!"

In seconds he was behind her, drawing her against him, clamping a hand over her mouth. And holding her so, he urged her along with him until he could slip his sword from his scabbard that lay on the earthen floor.

She saw the glistening steel held out inches from her face.

Raw panic filled her as the sound came again. Closer. Someone was out there; something was out there. She clenched her teeth together, trying not to let them chatter. She suddenly felt cold, as cold as ice, wondering. What was it, what strange forces had been borne upon the breeze, what unearthly power had touched her? And she knew, knew in her heart, that she had traveled through some strange void, perhaps a place where only God should tread himself. And now, no matter how she tried to deny these thoughts, she was so very terrified....

"Behind me!"

Her mouth was dry, she was frozen as he suddenly thrust her behind him again, ready to meet the danger that came their way.

Nearer, nearer, coming to the entrance of the cave.

Did he feel it? Had he known the same sensations? If he was afraid, he did not betray it, but stood ready, his sword glittering.

She braced behind him, and the rustling sound came louder.

Closer.

Louder...

CHAPTER FOUR

The sound stopped at last. They heard a dull click-ing. She realized that it was the slow movement of a horse's hooves, the animal approaching with care.

Vickie started to tremble, feeling the tension of the man before her.

Then it eased. Quickly, suddenly, completely.

"It's Max," he said, starting forward.

"Max?" Who the hell was Max? And how could Jason be so sure?

"I'll just get him."

"Don't you dare bring anyone in here!" Vickie cried, scrambling to get back into her clothing. But he had already stepped out—still stark naked—and he whistled, and then began to return.

"Jason—" she cried in fury and dismay.

"It's just my *horse!*" he assured her at last.

She had stumbled into her undergarments and had her dress over her head. In a second, helping hands were there along with her own. As her head came through the top of her dress, the first thing she saw was a handsome bay cavalry horse staring straight at her.

Max appeared just as authentic as his master, from his bridle to saddle pack. She'd seen dozens of horses that looked just like this one, in Gramps's old pic-

tures of the war. Max was the exact replica of a Confederate cavalry horse.

Or else, he actually was one.

It seemed that the ever-faithful mount with the keen
sense of smell had once again found his master—this
time through time!

Which made her wonder again if she might be the
one losing her mind. Was this her world—or his?
Could there really be a difference?

She didn't realize how long she had been staring at
the horse, pondering the question, until she saw that
Jason was dressed. His boots were on, and he was just
buckling his scabbard onto his hips. He was watching
her so intently that she inadvertently took a step back.

He strode over to her, capturing her hands, sweeping her back into his arms. He kissed her with a deep
passion so reminiscent of their lovemaking that she
found herself shuddering again, and remembering.
She barely knew him. Nine out of ten, he wasn't all
there. And she had just made love with him. And she
should be astounded with herself, horrified, and all
she knew was that...

His kiss made her long to lie down with him all over
again. The tension in his arms around her assured her
that he longed for the same. But his eyes, when they
rose over hers, were filled with pain.

"I have to find my brother," he said. "I have to."

She nodded. She refrained from telling him that it
had already been some time since he had found her,
and so it had been quite some time since he had left his
brother. If the man had been caught in the fire of a
battle, he had probably been discovered by someone
else. Or—he was dead.

"The rain—" she murmured.

"Has all but stopped. There's a bit of mist, that's all," he said.

She nodded again. He caught her hand again and led her, along with Max, out of the cave. The rain was a mist again. Delightfully cool against her face, when the days had been so atrociously hot.

He paused just outside the entrance to the cave. He touched her chin with his thumb and forefinger, raising it gently. She met the steady, silver-gray light of his eyes. She trembled slightly, afraid to close her own, afraid to be overtaken by a vision of his supple power, when he had held her, when he had made love to her.

The subtle curl of his lips was rueful. "I took you prisoner. I accused you of all manner of things."

"Yes, you did," she murmured in return.

"I'm sorry."

"You should be."

"Well, you're free now, you know."

Free? To her amazement, her heart did a double take. She couldn't possibly leave him. He could . . .

He could get hurt, she determined.

He was watching her so intently once again. She took a breath. Then she tossed back her hair and stared him down. "I'll help you find your brother," she said.

He was starting to mount his horse. "I don't want you hurt."

"And I don't want you arrested!" she sharply replied. "If you go stumbling around on this mountain and run into a twentieth-century cop, you're going to be in trouble!"

He had mounted his horse and was looking down at her. And she realized suddenly that she was furious. She'd been such a fool! Falling for this man, and now, insane or not, he was leaving her in the middle of nowhere after he'd imprisoned her for the night and...

And even managed to capture her heart.

"Oh! Go to hell!" she cried. "Surely that is the same for all worlds!"

She started to turn, but was amazed at the speed with which he leapt down, amazed at the vehemence with which he turned her to face him. "No!" she cried, finding herself in his arms once again, ready to beat against his chest. "No!" But the protest suddenly died on her lips as he held her and met her eyes. There was humor in his, and more. A myriad emotions she couldn't begin to determine, but she realized at last that one was concern.

"I don't know what I was thinking. I just wanted you to know that I wasn't...forcing you into being with me. But you're right. I can't let you go. You could stumble into real trouble."

"Me?"

"Into the midst of skirmishing," he told her.

"But—" She wanted to tell him that it hadn't been real. But how could she tell him that? She didn't want to believe, couldn't believe, *but she had felt the whistle of that bullet passing her cheek. She had felt it!* And it hadn't been just the bullets. It had been the blackness, the mist, the awful sense of fear, of the unknown.

They couldn't walk in and out of time! It was impossible. She closed her eyes, trying to remember exactly where they had been. The wind had been so fierce. . . .

All she could remember was a strangely bowed arbor of trees. And she couldn't quite remember where they had been.

No, they had stumbled upon reenactors, men taking the game just a bit too seriously.

His lips touched her forehead and he was setting her up on his horse, and leaping up behind her.

"Which way shall we try?" he murmured softly.

"South," she said, trying to rethink the battle. She should have known every phase of it. Blackfield's Mountain hadn't been nearly as big a battle as some of the others that the historians had really concentrated on—not like Gettysburg, Sharpsburg or Shiloh. And though the reenactment centered around the pasture where the main action had taken place, the battle had been in sets and maneuvers and skirmishes over a period of three days. She knew almost hourly day by day what had occurred. Gramps and his friends had written a guidebook for the interested tourist, and she had been enlisted to do much of the typing. The book was a very good one, she had heard from some of her military friends.

And if her memory wasn't failing her, there had been some troop movements south of the main mountain. There would be men displaying some cavalry skills today, women in costumes, all manner of activity.

Or else . . .

There might be a real battle.

"I think we should try straight south," she murmured. But the sky was still gray. She shook her head ruefully. "I really do have a sense of direction, and I do know this mountain, but—"

"South is that way," he said, pointing. He nudged Max. She rested her head back against his chest, and they started to ride. For a moment, neither of them spoke. There was a startling comfort in being together now, feeling the easy movement of Jason's horse carrying them down the mountain. There was warmth. A sense of belonging.

"So you say it's all over," he murmured suddenly. There was a light tone to his voice, but she was also convinced that there was deeper feeling there, too. Just as she was believing in him against all good sense, he was believing in her. His voice was suddenly pained and very husky. "And we lost, huh?"

She nodded, suddenly loath to say more.

"When does it end?"

"Well, there were still some troops in the field after, but most historians agree that it ended at Appomattox Courthouse, April of 1865."

"In 1865? Dear God, there's going to be that much more of this?"

The anguish in his voice touched her heart as nothing had before. There was so much else that would surely rip into his soul, once he knew the truth.

What was the truth?

"I wonder if I'll survive it," he mused suddenly. "And John. And so many others. Stonewall, Stuart, Lee—" He broke off suddenly. "You know, don't you?" he murmured.

"Lee comes through magnificently," she said quickly, loath to tell him about the others. "History has celebrated him as one of the greatest American generals—"

"Even though he lost?"

"Even though he lost. The children supposedly ran out into the streets to see him at Gettysburg. He was always a gentleman. He hated the bloodshed, and he was such an incredible military man, except for a very few mistakes. Pickett's Charge at Gettysburg—"

"Gettysburg?" he said, puzzled.

Of course. The action at Blackfield's Mountain had taken place in late summer, 1862. Gettysburg had taken place in July, 1863. To Jason, at this moment, Gettysburg was just an unknown tiny town in the North.

"Trust me. Lee remained deeply admired through all the decades," she murmured.

"And Stonewall?"

She didn't want to answer that question. And suddenly she didn't have to. They could hear shots, and a burst of fire. Jason reined in quickly, slipping down from Max. He haunched low, walking to the edge of the slope to look downward.

Vickie dismounted from Max in his wake. He turned back to her swiftly. "Stay there!"

She had no intention of doing so. She followed quickly to his side. She had barely reached him before he was shoving her behind him, and then down to the ground. They looked down the slope to the valley together.

Men in formation were marching toward one another. Yanks to the left, Rebs to the right. They were in nearly perfect, incredible lines, following orders. They marched, halted, loaded their weapons. Some men dropped to their knees while others shot above their heads from the ranks. Watching, Vickie felt the same amazement that she always did to watch such a battle. *How had anyone ever gotten men to stare at one another point-blank, so very close, and fire weapons? How had anyone ever gotten them to stand still when others were firing so closely at them?*

"They're so slow!" Jason murmured suddenly.

Another volley of fire burst out. Men in the Yankee ranks fell down.

Where were they? Were they real soldiers out there, fighting for their lives? Or was it the wonderfully accurate reenactment?

Then she saw *them*—the crowd lined up by the almost invisible wire fencing at the rear of the action. The viewers were on someone's cattle-grazing land, lined up at the fences to watch the spectacle.

She started to rise. His firm grasp was instantly upon her. "Get down!" he commanded her.

"It's all right!" she returned quickly. "They aren't real bullets."

"You might have said that before—"

"Look! Jason, look!" she implored him. Slow perhaps, but other than that, the reenactors looked so real. Seeing them, one could believe that it was really 1862.

But then there were the tourists at the fence. And there was the refreshment stand, painted bright red, with Coca-Cola emblazoned on it.

"There, Jason, look," she repeated softly.

And he did. He looked beyond the action to the crowd. To the drink stand. And he stared.

His gaze was completely stunned. If he had, indeed, come from a different world, she could easily understand his amazement. Things had changed. It was summer, and it was hot. Men were in T-shirts and cutoffs, women were in halter tops and shorts. Dozens of cars were parked in the field just behind the trees; someone beeped a horn and Jason winced. He kept staring.

More rifle fire went off. Men dropped on the Confederate side. The battle continued.

And Jason kept staring.

Then he turned away and sank back against the earth. Her eyes met his. He arched a brow to her, shaking his head slightly. "They aren't wearing any clothes."

She smiled. "Honest, they're dressed quite respectably by today's standards."

"Fashion has... progressed."

He was speaking lightly. He was dazed, of course. Then she realized his concern when he spoke with a hollow anguish. "How the hell do I get back? If I don't, John will die."

They hadn't been watching. Now there was a sudden burst of applause. The reenactment program for the day had ended. The "dead" men were rising. Friends were talking, some people were walking toward their cars and some were walking toward the hills that hid the encampments from view.

She reached out, slipping her hand into his. "If we can get down there for now, I can get us something to eat. And we can go home. And maybe Gramps will have something to say that will help you somehow."

His eyes caught hers. He shook his head, still fighting his amazement.

"It has to help to have a decent meal!" she encouraged him.

At last he stood, bringing her with him to her feet. She curled her fingers around his. They started down the slope, Max trailing behind them.

Vickie had forgotten just how hungry she was until she began to smell food. The scent drove her nearly to distraction, but some warning bell went off in her head before they reached the crowd. She stopped, turning quickly, placing a hand against Jason's chest.

"Wait."

"What?"

"You can't just go down there and tell people—you can't run around telling people that you're from the real battle."

His eyes narrowed sharply at her.

"They won't believe you!"

His jaw set firmly. "It's the truth."

"But you can't say that it is. Don't you understand? I know they had asylums in your day—do you want to wind up in one?"

He was still staring at her. She clutched his arm. "This is my world!" she hissed to him. "You have to behave in it, or they'll cart you away. They'll never believe you."

He stared out over her head, trying to take in the twentieth-century world.

Then his gaze riveted upon hers. "Do you believe me?"

She hesitated the briefest moment. She believed with her whole heart that he meant what he said. And though it now seemed something of a blur, she could easily enough convince herself that the fighting up on the mountain earlier had been real. It had been a real bullet to nearly graze her cheek.

"Yes," she said suddenly, and it was the first time she really admitted it to herself. "I believe you."

He blinked. His lips curled into a slow smile. He bowed to her. "Then I am yours to command, Victoria. I shall behave however you bid."

Her eyes locked with his. She smiled, too. "For the moment, just keep quiet and I'll get us some hot dogs."

"You folks eat dog?"

She shook her head vehemently. "Sausages! They're like sausages. Can't you smell them? Aren't you starving? Come on!"

He stared downward once again. Parking hadn't been allowed very near the soldiers' camps, but there were cars in the field behind the trucks, past the battle site. Vickie saw that he was dead still, studying them gravely.

"Cars. Horseless carriages."

His eyes shot to hers. "How do they run?"

"On gas. Fuel. I don't really understand it myself."

"They're new?"

"Invented right around the turn of the century," Vickie said.

He started walking.

"You can't go inspecting cars! I have one at home. I'll try to explain it to you. Please, please act normally!" Vickie beseeched Jason.

He sighed and looked down at her. "I'll try," he promised. "But don't you see? Nothing is normal."

She bit her lip and nodded. *"Try."*

She hurried forward. He lagged behind her. She realized that there were more new sights he was staring at. More than just the cars parked in the field. The power poles rising far down the road. The people all around them. The reenactor Yanks now laughing with the reenactor Rebs.

"Please be careful," she warned him again.

He nodded. She held his arm, more or less leading him through the crowd.

They reached the stand. There was a girl in front of Vickie who ordered a soda and a hot dog and moved on. Jason watched her with keen interest. Vickie's stomach growled with hunger, but then she remembered that she didn't have any money with her, not a cent.

She backed away suddenly. "What's the matter?" Jason asked. He was blending in perfectly, she thought. People were staring at him, but they were all smiling, assuming he was part of the show. In turn, he politely inclined his head.

"I don't have any money with me," she said. "We'll—"

"I have money," he said. He stepped around her. "Two of those, please. And two of the drinks." He reached into a small waistband pocket of his pants where he kept a small fold of bills.

Confederate bills, Vickie realized.

"No!" she cried suddenly. She caught hold of his hands, trying to lower them before the man could see them. "Let's not have hot dogs."

Now everyone was staring at her. The balding hot-dog vendor, the people around her, Jason. "They're really not very healthy. They're awful for your cholesterol level."

"Your *what?*" Jason demanded.

More people were gathering around them. "Vickie, will you let me buy the things?" he said with exasperation. "You ran down here, craving one so deeply."

"I've changed my mind." Her fingers tightened around his. "Besides, this is really highway robbery. They're two-fifty apiece. *Two-fifty in American money.* Greenbacks. U.S. money. Federal money."

"Highway robbery?" the vendor protested. "Lady, these are good dogs. Mile-long dogs, all-beef, and they're kosher, as well!"

"If you don't want a hot dog," a little boy behind them said eagerly, "I do."

"We don't," Vickie said quickly. She caught Jason's wrist, pulling him from the line. And once they were outside it, she tried to explain in a rushed whisper, "You can't use Confederate money."

"It's worthless?"

"Yes. Well, actually, people collect it now, so it might be worth a great deal. But you can't buy hot dogs with it."

"Because we lost," he said softly, silver-gray eyes level, enigmatic, upon her.

She nodded.

"Vickie! There you are!"

She whirled around. Steve, clad in his Yankee blue, was hurrying toward them. She felt Jason stiffen at her side.

"He's a friend! And the war is over!" she hissed to Jason. "Steve!" she greeted her friend. "I didn't know that you were taking part in this skirmishing."

"Well, it must be because you didn't ask," he told her. He flung an arm around her shoulders and gave her a hug.

She was startled to feel a firm hand on her arm. Jason's. Drawing her back against him. And he was staring at Steve with a silver fire in his eyes.

"Hello," Steve said curiously to him.

"Steve, this is Jason."

"Colonel Tarkenton," Jason said.

Vickie gritted her teeth. "Jason, this is a very good friend of mine, Steve Hanson. He and my late husband went to school together."

"Nice to meet you," Steve said, looking over Jason with obvious curiosity. It was all she needed at the moment. Steve taking on a big-brother attitude. Jason behaving as if . . .

As if she was his woman. Well, just what impression had she given him?

"Where do you hail from—Colonel Tarkenton?" Steve asked politely.

"Virginia, but pretty far southwest from here. A little place past Staunton."

"Nice country over there, too."

"Beautiful. Thanks."

"You didn't go to GWU, too, did you?"

"Pardon?"

"To school?"

"Oh. I attended West Point. That was before the current difficulty, of course."

"The current difficulty?" Steve said blankly.

"The war, sir, the war!"

"Always in character!" Vickie murmured. "That's what makes these things so wonderful. You're just all so very...involved."

"Oh, right—the current difficulty," Steve said, and then he laughed.

Maybe they were thawing a little.

And maybe Steve had some money to lend her.

"Steve! Can I borrow ten dollars?" she asked quickly.

Jason stiffened as if he had been slapped, but Vickie ignored him. She was too hungry to go through the whole money conversation again, and certainly couldn't argue with Jason over it in front of Steve.

"Ten dollars? Sure," Steve said, laughing. He reached into an inside pocket of the Federal-issue jacket he was wearing and produced his wallet. He pulled out a bill, but Jason's hand fell on his before he could pass it to her.

"She can't take that, sir," he said firmly.

"Yes, she can!" Vickie insisted. She could already taste a delicious, cholesterol-filled hot dog this very moment.

"It's just ten dollars—" Steve began.

"Nevertheless, she can't just take it."

"But she can—" Vickie began insistently, yet she never got the chance to finish. She found herself drawn somewhat behind Jason Tarkenton and he was producing his Confederate notes, out of the Bank of Virginia. "We can't spend these," Jason said. "But I understand they're worth something. Can we trade?"

Steve stared from the bills to Jason's face incredulously. Very tentatively, he took one. Then he shook his head, staring at Jason again. "These are real."

"Well, of course they're real, sir! I'm certainly no counterfeiter."

Vickie kicked him. "What?" Steve said, frowning.

"Boys, boys, you do take this all so seriously!" Vickie piped up quickly. Jason cast her one of his warning silver-gray stares. But Steve smiled a little bit sheepishly.

"Yeah, sometimes we do." He studied the note he had taken from Jason with fascination. Then he handed it back. "I'm not a collector in this field, but this is definitely worth more than ten dollars. I can't take it from you."

"Then we can't take your ten, sir," Jason said with a ring of steel to his voice.

We! Where did this "we" come in? She could *gladly* take the darned ten dollars. She was just about ready to kill for a hot dog!

"Steve! Please take the bill for ten," she begged.

"But he can't be serious," Steve said.

"But he is! *Please?*" she implored him.

Steve finally shrugged. "I hate to think I've taken advantage of anyone—"

"You're not." She slipped the ten from Steve's fingers. Jason pressed his Confederate bill back into Steve's hand.

She was grateful to see that there was no line now at the hot-dog truck. "Two, please! And two Cokes."

The hot-dog vendor remembered her. "I wouldn't want to rip you off, lady," he said pointedly.

"Please! Give me a hot dog!"

The vendor shook his head, muttering to himself. He delivered her the two hot dogs and sodas. She paid him, juggled everything to bring the food and drinks back to Jason.

To her dismay, she saw that another friend had joined Steve. And the three of them had gotten into a discussion over the battle that had been fought here today.

"Hell, Steve, he's right. This battle was a Confederate victory. History may call it something of a stalemate, but think about it. The Yanks had two-thirds more men. They were well supplied. The Rebs were trying to reach their supply line, and they were outnumbered two to one. It should have been all over except that Stonewall did rally more troops in," Steve's friend was saying.

And Jason was just staring at the man, trying to comprehend how the fellow in the Yankee blue could be on his side in the argument.

"They lost nearly equal numbers—" Steve began stubbornly.

"They routed the Yanks," his friend said.

"They were better horsemen," Jason said suddenly.

Everyone stopped and stared at him. He smiled ruefully. "We—" He caught Vickie's eyes. "They, I mean, were simply much better horsemen. Southerners were raised to hunt, to ride, to race. In a situation like this, they were able to ride a few circles around the Yanks."

"See? Exactly my point!" Steve's friend said excitedly. "Oh, the Yanks did have some good fellows. Custer did damned well at Gettysburg—"

"Who?" Jason inquired.

"George Armstrong Custer. He—"

"That cutup?" Jason said incredulously.

"What?"

Vickie slammed down on Jason's foot. He shook his head, frowning at her. "Custer really was a wretched student. That's in the records—I imagine. Sorry, go on."

"Custer sure held up Stuart at Gettysburg. But then again, it was the first real bad time that Lee had to work without Stonewall—"

"Without Stonewall?" Jason said.

"Sure. He was dead before Gettysburg, you know. And as to Custer, well he met his unhappy end in 1877, right? Took a lot of men with him, but it seems lots of folks—all Yanks by that time—thought that he acted such a brazen fool he all but deserved it himself."

Jason stared at him blankly.

"The Battle of the Little Bighorn," Vickie said briefly, smiling. But Jason wasn't thinking about Custer. He was still assimilating the fact that Stonewall Jackson had been killed.

Vickie thrust a hot dog and drink into Jason's hand and slipped a finally free hand around his arm. "We've got to go," she said, searching her mind for a reason. She found one. A real one. "I—er—I've been gone a lot longer than I intended. Gramps is going to be very worried. Come on, Jason. We've got to see him!"

He followed her lead, but she could see that his face had turned somewhat pale.

"Hey, nice horse, Tarkenton!" Steve called after him. "You've really done it all right!"

Vickie waved cheerily. She urged Jason along. "This way. I know where I am now. My home is right over the next rise."

The hot dogs she had wanted so badly were still in their hands, untouched. She had at least managed to steer him away from the crowd. But even as they started up the rise, he pulled back.

"Stonewall?" he demanded.

She hesitated. "He was killed by one of his own pickets. Well, mortally wounded." She hesitated, biting into her lower lip.

He sank to the ground, sitting, staring back at the milling people. "It's a game. It's nothing more than a game to them. All those people gave so much! Fought and bled and died, and it's nothing more than a game to them!"

She stared down at him, seeing for a moment the bewilderment on his features, and then the anger.

And then she felt a little anger of her own taking root.

"No! No, it's much, much more than a *game!* Don't you see that? It's *history.* It's remembering, it's keeping the heartache and the pain alive. It's a way of honoring all that happened then. You shouldn't be angry. You should be grateful. No man who fought died in vain. Not Yanks, not Rebels. You tested our nation. You broke it apart. You fought and died, and in the end, over time, you made it whole, you made it strong. What happened probably had to happen so that we could meet the twentieth century with the strength needed to survive, to arise a world power. There's so much that you don't know. How can you fairly judge us?"

He set his hot dog and soda down on the ground and stood with a sudden vehemence that frightened her. Maybe she had been wrong to forget that he might be a madman.

Maybe she had really been a fool to contradict him so bluntly.

He walked toward her with his silver eyes glittering. A soft cry escaped her and she started backing away. He reached toward her. Lifted the food from her hands and set it down with purpose.

"Keep your distance, now," she demanded. "I'm warning you—"

He paused for a minute, silver eyes searing as they touched upon hers. "Oh?" he said softly. "Warning me? And just what are you going to do?"

She clenched her teeth together for a moment, staring him down. "I'm going to eat my damned hot dog, that's what I'm going to do! I'll just leave you to wallow in your self-pity, and eat my hot dog, since you've managed to starve me rather nicely! Then I'm going home!"

He took another step toward her. "I'm sorry!" she cried. "I'm sorry for the horrible things that you're learning. But I can't change them, and I can't stop everyone else from telling you the truth. I still can't even really believe that this can be the truth, but I do believe you and I—I care about you and . . . stop!"

But neither warnings nor threats seemed to mean anything to him. He caught her by the shoulders. Wrenched her into his arms. Kissed her. Deeply. With that same passion that had made her forget everything except how much she wanted him. She wanted to protest; she stiffened in his arms at first. But the liquid fire of his kiss was overwhelming, and her hands fell upon his arms when they should have been beating against him.

Then she found her head leaned against his chest, his hands stroking over her hair. "It is a world gone mad," he said softly. "A nightmare. Yet you are in it." And his eyes touched her. "Wild, brash, brave. A touch of magic." His knuckles moved over her cheek.

Magic. Yes, that was it. He was magic himself....

And she was suddenly afraid. Very afraid. Magic could vanish. And she was allowing herself to become so intensely involved. Touched. Loved...

"We have to go," she said breathlessly. "My grandfather will be frightfully worried. Please..."

"Let's go, then." He set her drink and her hot dog back in her hands. "Wherever you shall lead, I will follow," he told her, silver-gray eyes shimmering into hers. "For the moment," he added softly.

"For the moment?"

"Don't you see, Victoria? I'm lost. I've got to find my way back. To John."

"Your brother."

"Yes, my brother. I promised him that I'd come back to him, Vickie."

"But what if there isn't a way?"

He shook his head. "There has to be a way. I've lost so much, Vickie. John is all I have left. And I promised him."

She bit her lip, watching him with a sudden flicker of tears stinging her eyes. She understood that.

Gramps. He was the someone she had left.

"There's a secret locked in the mountain up there," he persisted. "There's an archway, between the trees.

I know it's there—I just have to find it again. Max stumbled through it. We stumbled through it. And left it once again."

"You don't know that—"

"I know it. And you know it. No one involved in one of your *reenactments* would have been shooting real bullets at us, right? I have to go back. But I am exhausted and starving—and grateful to you." He hesitated a moment, then stroked her cheek once again. She felt the breeze touch them then, too. Against the heat of the sun, it was cool, light, as soft as that stroke of his flesh. "Grateful, and much, much more!" he murmured, his tone husky, and very low. Then he continued, the soldier, the man, his voice growing deeper. "I want to see you home, and accept your help. Maybe in this world of modern wonders, there is something that I could bring back to save my brother. So, please," he said very softly, "lead forward."

CHAPTER FIVE

Vickie decided it was best if she first saw Gramps alone, so Jason waited at the roadside. As she walked up to the house, her heart was pounding with a sudden ferocity. Gramps was so old now, he was all that she had and he was probably worried sick!

She burst into the house, calling his name. "Gramps? Gramps? Where are you?"

The door to the taproom stood to her right, and the curving hallway to the bedrooms just upstairs was in front of her. She didn't know which way to run first.

"Gramps!"

The taproom door burst open and he came through, blue eyes wild and anxious.

"Vickie! Victoria! Where in tarnation have you been, young woman? When your horse came back without you last night, I'd have died with worry if I hadn't been so afraid!"

"I'm sorry, Gramps, so very sorry!" She linked her arms around his neck, hugging him fiercely, kissing his weathered cheek and then hugging him again. Where had she been? What story was she going to give him?

And just how was she going to explain Jason Tarkenton?

"The weather, Gramps," she said quickly. "There were the strangest storms on the peaks. Arabesque threw me and I'm afraid that I became horribly disoriented walking in the dark last night and—''

She broke off. Her grandfather's hold on her had stiffened and he was looking over her shoulder.

He was looking at Jason. And Max.

Why hadn't he waited, as they'd agreed? She had left the front door open when she came in the house and now Jason stood just outside, one foot on the first step, his handsome cavalry mount behind him. Jason had heard every word that she'd said, and now he was coming up the steps.

"I thought you went to see Yankees, girl?" Gramps asked softly.

"Yes, well, I did go to see my Yank friends," she said lightly. "But I ran into a Rebel on my way home." Oh, dear God, get her through this! she thought. She pulled away from her grandfather, trying to smile broadly. "Gramps, this is an old friend. Jason Tarkenton. He hasn't been able to find any lodging so I've brought him home for the night. It will only take a minute to fix up one of the guest rooms. He's, umm, he's been looking after me, it seems, since—lately. I knew you'd be happy to have him here." Was that close to the truth? Not in the least. And Jason wasn't going to let it go by.

Damn him!

He was now standing in the doorway. "My deepest apologies, sir. That your granddaughter was waylaid was entirely my fault, and I do beg your pardon. I'm deeply sorry for all the anxiety I've put you through."

Gramps looked from Jason to Vickie, arching a brow slowly. He looked their visitor over with a deliberate curiosity. He cast Vickie a glance of pure suspicion. Then he extended a hand to Jason. "How do you do, sir? An old friend of my granddaughter's, eh?"

"Yes," Vickie said.

"That's not exactly true," Jason told him. "As I said, the fact that she was waylaid was entirely my fault. But I swear to you, sir, that I mean to honor our relationship."

Vickie winced. *Honor* their relationship?

She wanted to strangle him. But Gramps was still staring at them both with wonder.

"I swear it, sir," Jason told Gramps.

"Mmm—that chili smells delicious!" Vickie cried out. She needed to have a talk with Jason. A long talk. But for now, she'd just have to try and distract Gramps. "Gramps, please tell me that we've some chili left. I'm absolutely starving."

Gramps was still staring at Jason. "You been eating hardtack, huh?" he said.

It didn't sound as if he were teasing.

"An awful lot of it sir. And I just tried a hot dog, too."

"Gramps, will you excuse me for a moment? I need to speak with Jason alone outside for just a minute."

"You waylaid her, eh?" Gramps said.

She shoved against Jason's chest. He wasn't moving. "Yes, sir. I needed help. But I swear to you as a gentleman that I mean to protect her honor and—"

"Jason, may I please speak with you outside?"

"There's been more to this than a walk in the woods," Gramps said to Jason.

"Yes, sir."

"Jason! Gramps, you will excuse me!" She pushed with all her power against Jason's chest. He still didn't move. He obviously believed that this discussion was between him and Gramps. He wasn't budging, and he was muscled like steel. And Gramps wasn't politely moving away, either.

She decided to talk anyway. "This is the twentieth century! I'm not one of your long-ago *possession-type* females. I make my own decisions! I'm not dishonored in any way, shape or form, and you don't *owe* me anything. And quite frankly, I'd truly appreciate it if you could manage not to be so damned *honorable* for a while, here! I resent being *owed* whatever it is you think that you owe me."

"Possession types?" he said, eyes intense, his voice very low, and sounding something like a growl.

"Yes! As if women are automatically things that you have to take responsibility for—"

"Let him be responsible!" Gramps chimed in.

"My females, Victoria, are not *possessions!*" Jason informed her. "They think, they feel, they weigh matters and they make decisions. But, Jesu, lady, they know how to listen, too, how to be cherished, how to love and cherish in return. And they also respect and honor the men in their lives!"

Suddenly—and a little bit too late—it seemed that Gramps had heard what she had said before and was anxious that the two of them get something to eat. "Chili's on!" he announced jovially. "Come on into the taproom, you two, and we'll see if we can't cool down your tempers by heating up your appetites. This is an unexpected ripple in the day, by golly!"

Oh, it was a ripple, all right, Vickie thought. She tried to control both her temper and her nervousness, giving Jason a very stern stare.

He ignored her, of course.

They followed him in. Gramps walked around the counter to the kitchen area. "Pour your man an ale, Victoria," Gramps commanded.

She gritted her teeth. "He isn't *my man*, Gramps. He's a friend." She stared at Jason very hard. "And I'm trying very hard to help him!" She dropped her voice for Jason alone. "You're making it very difficult!" she rasped beneath her breath.

He returned her stare and spoke softly. "I can *try* to behave, Victoria, but I can't change what I am."

Gramps, pulling a microwave container out of the refrigerator and slipping it into the microwave, grinned back. "Sounds interesting, anyway. You scared me half to death, young lady. I was ready to call in the FBI."

Vickie pulled the tap down for a draft beer for Jason, and then decided to have one herself.

She needed one.

She walked around the bar and saw that Jason was staring at what Gramps was doing. She realized then that the microwave and the refrigerator must be absolute wonders to him—not to mention the electric lights.

She set a beer down before him, and narrowed her eyes at him, trying desperately to warn him that he must be careful.

"Here we are!" Gramps said.

Jason's brows arched. "That fast? Cooked food that fast?"

She didn't think that Gramps had heard. "The world has been in an age of invention, almost since the war ended," she said, speaking incredibly quickly. "That's a refrigerator and freezer. It runs off electricity and keeps things cold. That's a microwave oven. I don't know exactly how microwaves work, but it cooks food very, very fast."

Almost as fast as she had been speaking, she thought with a wince. Jason couldn't have grasped too much of what she had said. But it didn't matter; she couldn't repeat anything. Gramps was on his way over with the chili now. Setting it down before them with plates and utensils and napkins. "Thanks, Vickie, I'll just get my own beer," Gramps said reproachfully.

She cast him a hard gaze. "You didn't say that you wanted one!" she reminded him, and she quickly went to pour a third beer, trying to keep her eye on the two men.

"You've been out for a while," Gramps said. "Bet you could use a nice hot bath and a change of clothing. After keeping my granddaughter out all that time."

"Gramps!"

"Sir, I've told you—"

"May I see that sword you've got there, Mr. Tarkenton?" Gramps asked suddenly.

"Of course."

Jason stood instantly and Vickie bit into her lower lip. He'd lost his plumed hat along the way and was clad only in his cavalry shirt, breeches and boots, but he wore them so exceptionally well. He was as lean and hard as any fighter, striking and agile as he drew his sword from its scabbard. Her heart seemed to catapult and spread as she watched him, fascinated by his movement, by the unruly length of his tawny hair, by the silver fire in his eyes and the hard-set determination in every line and plane of his face.

He walked his sword around to Gramps, who took it far more reverently than it had been offered.

Gramps studied the sword and Vickie held her breath. He looked up at Jason at last. "It's real!" he said in a whisper. "This thing is a real Confederate cavalry officer's sword, out of Richmond. I've never seen such a fine example. And the scabbard. It's real, too?"

Jason unbuckled his scabbard and handed it over, too. Gramps looked into his eyes, then to the scabbard. After a moment he said with certain wonder, "My God. This thing is in excellent shape. There's some slashes in the leather—"

"That one was Manassas," Jason said, leaning over.

Vickie tried to kick him unobtrusively. She managed to get his shin. He stared at her hard, brows knitting into a frown.

"Gramps," she admonished, still staring at Jason, "quit being such a historian, huh? Let the poor man eat his chili."

"Right. Go ahead, young man. Dig in. It's just that I'm a collector, you know. And an armchair historian. Well, I used to reenact, too, but the old bones are getting a little sore for sleeping out in tents and such. This is one of the finest pieces I've ever seen, including any I've seen in the top museums!"

"Er... thank you," Jason murmured.

"Eat your chili, son."

Jason did. Vickie realized that he must have been starving by then—*really* starving—because he tried to start slowly, but in a matter of minutes, he was eating as fast as his hand could carry his spoon from the plate to his mouth. And of course, she was starving herself. She ate quickly, too. And Gramps was silent until their spoons clinked against their bowls.

"That was excellent," Jason said quietly. "Thank you very much. It was truly the best meal I've had in—" He broke off. "Ages," he finished limply, watching Vickie.

Gramps grunted, still studying him. "It was a bowl of chili. Good recipe, but just chili. You haven't been eating very well lately, have you, Mr. Tarkenton?"

Vickie felt a twinge of real unease. Gramps just didn't intend to let her get away with this. She wished she could just tell him the truth.

Or what she thought she believed to be the truth!

"Gramps, really! My guest's eating habits—"

"Are darned curious, darned curious," Gramps finished. "So, let's see now, did you and Victoria go to school together, too?"

"Yes," Vickie lied.

"No," Jason said simultaneously.

"No!" Vickie said quickly, but Jason was in the process of changing his response to an emphatic, "Yes, sir!"

"Right," Gramps said, nodding gravely. "Where do you come from, Mr. Tarkenton?"

Vickie opened her mouth to answer quickly for him.

Gramps was quicker.

"Now, Victoria, I asked Mr. Tarkenton."

Jason grinned. He liked Gramps a lot, she could see that. Gramps was going to get right to any point.

"I come from a little town just west of Staunton."

"And your folks have been from around there for a long time, I take it?"

"That's right, sir. Late 1700s."

"Which is it? You did or didn't go to school with Vickie?"

"Didn't, sir."

"You attended college?"

"West Point."

"Gramps, can we please play Twenty Questions later?" Vickie said. "Jason needs a bath and some sleep—"

"Why?" Gramps asked her, wide-eyed.

"We were up all night," she said. "Trying to get back."

"Oh, yeah, right," Gramps said. "Where are your things, Mr. Tarkenton? You didn't ride your horse all the way up here from the Staunton area, did you?"

"Of course he didn't!" Vickie exclaimed quickly.

"What, did you trailer him on in for the reenactment?"

"Yes," Vickie answered.

"Let Mr. Tarkenton answer himself. That is, if you don't mind, Mr. Tarkenton," Gramps said.

But Jason, it seemed, did mind something. His eyes were steady on Gramps, his jaw was set. "I'll answer whatever you like. But let's get this settled. It's either Jason, sir, or Colonel Tarkenton. *Colonel* Tarkenton."

Gramps's brows shot up. Vickie would have kicked Jason beneath the table again—really hard—except that he stood then, not allowing her to do so.

Then Gramps was on his feet himself. "All right, *Colonel* Tarkenton, just where do you really come from?"

"The Staunton area!" Jason said.

"Then just why is everything about you so damned different? And why is it that you've been staring at the lights and the refrigerator and microwave as if you just walked off a spaceship?"

"A spaceship?" Jason said. He looked at Vickie, frowning. "A spaceship?"

She smiled suddenly. She'd always known that Gramps was sharp as nails, but she'd never imagined that things could get this difficult.

One thing she knew for certain, though, and she should have realized it from the beginning. No matter what she told him—and whether he believed her or not—he wouldn't act against her in any way. She was going to have to put some faith in him.

Either that, or gag Jason. She wasn't sure that that was possible.

She felt like laughing hysterically. She actually smiled at Jason. "A spaceship. You know, flying around in outer space. Men have walked on the moon, you see."

He shook his head. *"Men have walked on the moon?"*

She nodded gravely, still smiling. This was so ridiculous. There were moments when she couldn't fathom the fact that she had decided to believe all this herself. She looked at her grandfather.

"He's from the war, Gramps. The real one."

Gramps sank into his chair quickly, staring up at Jason. "'The war. The real one,'" he repeated.

"Before God, sir, it's the truth," Jason said. He spoke softly, but there was a passion in his voice that rang sincere. Gramps stared at Vickie. She stared back.

He shook his bald head, at a loss. "How?" he said at last. "You know... that just can't be."

"But it is," Jason assured him. "And I don't know how, not exactly. I think that there is some kind of a doorway within the arch of a number of trees. I think that I've been through it twice, and I'm convinced that I can find it again. I don't think I really believe all of this myself, except that I've come from a raging battle to see dozens of *horseless* carriages lined up in a field. Now I've seen strange lights and that thing you call a refrigerator or freezer. It really can't be true. I don't believe any of it—except that it's happened to me."

Gramps was just staring at him. Vickie held her breath. Then Gramps began to speak slowly. "If such a thing were going to happen—and I'm not saying for a minute that it has—the time would be right. These are the exact same days in which the battle and skirmishes were fought all those years ago. They've even fallen the same—Sunday is Sunday, and so forth. The weather is the same, the place is the same," Gramps murmured. "And there were storms. Strange and powerful electrical storms, like we're having now. So maybe, if a door were to open, it would open now."

"So you believe him?" Vickie breathed.

"I didn't say that at all!" Gramps warned her. He stared at Jason, frowning. "By the saints!" he muttered suddenly. "If what you're telling me is true, then . . . to you, it has all just begun. Stonewall is yet to come in to fight here. He's yet to—"

"Die," Jason said flatly.

"And the war—"

"Is yet to be lost," Jason finished.

Gramps nodded. "I'm sorry, young fellow. Truly sorry."

"I'm going to go back," Jason said. "I'm going to find the passageway. It exists. I was there, I *know* I was there. But we were outnumbered, and Vickie was with me. I didn't dare stay. But I must go back."

Gramps was shaking his head suddenly, vehemently.

"No. The South loses. It would be foolish for you to go back. And maybe that passageway is gone now. Have you thought of that? It has to be an extraordinary happening. If such things do open, then they must close, too."

Vickie clenched her teeth suddenly, fighting the chill that had seized her. There were moments when she truly questioned her sanity and wondered if she had imagined the events on the mountainside. There couldn't really be Yankees; they couldn't really have been shooting at her.

But even that battlefield hadn't been as frightening as the feel of the wind. Gramps was right—if there was a passageway from one time to another, it certainly was extraordinary. And if it opened—it would close. It was filled with a strange, dangerous violence, with a wild wind, with a frightening, gripping chill. It had seemed to enclose her as if it wanted to hold her there, in the wind and wicked darkness, forever.

She stared at Jason and spoke very softly, "Gramps is right. The South loses. What is there for you to go back for? Think about it, Jason. There's nothing back there except for fear and horror and…maybe death."

"I have to go back," Jason said firmly.

Gramps arched a brow high. "You've got a wife?" he said suspiciously.

"My wife is dead."

"Don't go back," Gramps insisted.

"He's right!" Vickie cried. "What's back there for you? Loss and pain. You can't change things—"

"Maybe I can."

They were all silent for a minute. Maybe he *could* change things, with what he knew now.

And what would that mean?

"You can't—tamper—with history."

"I *have* to go back. My brother is caught on that mountain, somewhere back in time, dying."

"Wounded?" Gramps said.

Jason nodded. Gramps drummed his fingers on the table. Then he jumped up suddenly. "Maybe you can do something. Maybe you can't. It's darn sure, though, that you can't find your way back now. Dusk is almost here, and it goes black on the mountaintop after that. I've got to go out. Vickie, let him finish his beer. Draw him a nice hot bath. Give him some clean clothing to wear. I'll be back by the time you're both spruced up."

"Where are you going?" Vickie demanded.

"To the library. And now, you— Never mind! I'll see you soon. Real soon." He started out, but paused at the door, looking back. "I'm not saying I believe a word of this, you know!"

Then he was gone. Vickie stared after him, then hurried to catch up. She left the taproom, came back into the entry of the house and stood by the screen door.

There was Gramps, patting Max on the nose. She felt Jason behind her. They both watched while Gramps inspected Max's feet, then patted him on the nose again.

"What is he doing?" Vickie murmured softly.

"Looking at the way he's shod. Inspecting the saddle and the saddlebags. He's a smart old fellow," Jason said. He was quiet for a minute. "Imagine. He believed in me right away," he said softly.

Vickie swung around. He was standing so close behind her that she was less than an inch away from him when she faced him. His warmth seemed to flood over her. She could feel the magical energy of his strength, feel his heat. He was impossible, unerringly courteous, so damned protective, it was irritating. No, it wasn't really irritating. It was different. And if she admitted it, she had been loved like that once before. Maybe it had been the twentieth century, but Brad had loved her like that, the way in which he cast himself between her and danger at all times. She was a twentieth-century woman, but that feeling of being cherished was a good one.

And maybe it didn't matter, with a man, just what era he'd come from. Jason Tarkenton was stubborn, set and determined.

But she didn't want him to go away. It was incredible. He had become so very much to her so quickly.

She swallowed hard. He *was* going back, with first light. When he could find his archway through time. No matter how extraordinary—or frightening—it was. And she had to let him go. He came from a world where battle still roared. He had lived all of his life believing that honor and loyalty were everything. She couldn't stop him from going.

And neither could she be sorry that he had come.

"Gramps is very special," she said quietly. "I owe him everything. He has always been there for me." She was suddenly convinced that she would burst into the strangest outpouring of tears if she wasn't careful. She pushed against his chest, determined to get by him. "I'll get some clothes for you. Brad was about your size—"

"Brad?"

"My husband. There's a bathroom at the top of the stairs, towels are in the linen closet in the hallway. Go on up and I'll find you something. If you're going to go back, you can leave with a full stomach, a hot bath and a good night's sleep behind you. Maybe that will help you change history."

He was staring at her. He winced, and she saw the pain and worry in his eyes. She knew that he was feeling a certain guilt for having strayed so far from his brother.

But she knew, too, that he was also fascinated by the time that he was spending with her.

"Jason!" she murmured suddenly.

"Yes?"

"You've got to start—"

A tawny brow arched high. "I've got to start what?" he demanded.

"I'm not helpless. I can take care of myself. You have to start being—careful."

"Meaning?"

"You don't have to protect me so much, that's all."

He lifted her chin, staring into her blue eyes. "I can't change the truth, and I'm sorry. I found it impossible to lie to a man like your grandfather—and I'm sorry again. Where I come from, we honor our commitments."

"But you can't honor anything, don't you see?" Vickie whispered. "Because you're going back!"

He stepped away from her. Maybe that was a truth that he had never seen. "I have to," he murmured painfully.

No! Vickie's heart seemed to cry. There had to be a way for him *not* to go back.

He suddenly lifted a piece of hair from her face, smoothing his knuckles over her cheek.

"Then there's nothing to honor."

"Maybe there is."

"How—?"

"You could come back with me," he said.

"What?" she barely formed the word.

He smiled. "I guess not. I'm going back to a war—and a country that loses that war. And through... through that tunnel. You've got hot dogs and microwaves. It would be incredibly foolish, wouldn't it?" He paused a moment, then brushed her lips tenderly with his. "This bathroom of yours is at the top of the stairs?" he asked.

She nodded. He turned around then and silently followed the instructions she had given him before, walking up the stairs to the second floor of the house.

She let out a long breath, watched him go and then hurried up the stairs behind him.

Take care of things, she thought. Don't think!

She had given most of Brad's things to charities when he had been killed, but there were still a number of his jeans and shirts in the back bedroom. She didn't sleep there. She hadn't slept near anything of his once he had died, not since the night she had cried all night because she'd had one of his shirts in her hands. That had been a long time ago now. She could do this.

She found a comfortable worn pair of light blue jeans and a tailored cotton shirt in a soft warm maroon. She walked down the hall to the front bathroom and suddenly heard an oath explode.

"Jesu!"

There was a burst of water.

She knocked lightly and opened the door. He was stripped of his uniform with a white towel knotted around his waist and for a second it seemed that her heart stopped, then plummeted onward again. Bronzed and so taut-muscled. She felt a flare of color rushing to her cheeks. She itched to touch him. Longed to open her mouth and say that she was so very afraid that she had missed something before, could she please inspect him from head to toe.

He didn't seem to notice that she was staring at him. "How do you manage these damned things?" he inquired of the faucets.

She smiled, and turned them both down. "Bath or shower?" she asked him.

A spark touched his eyes. His lips curled up slowly. "Well, I don't know. That depends. Are you joining me or not?" His hands were upon her. Touching her shoulders. Drawing her near to him. And then his mouth was on hers. She could feel the fire burning his flesh, the strength in his fingers. She stroked his arms, his chest, felt the fever seep like lava into her body, warming her, with each liquid sweep and caress of his tongue.

Oh, yes ... !

He drew her closer and closer, molding her to his length. She could feel the muscled pressure of his thighs against hers, despite the towel, despite her dress. She could feel more. Insinuative, explicit, exciting. The rise of his desire, hard and pressing, against her. Sweetness reaching around her, creating a stirring hunger. She returned his kiss, hungry, wanting more....

She could feel the tension that suddenly gripped his body. The shudder that seemed to shake him from head to toe.

And he groaned, deep in his throat.

And then suddenly, he was pressing her away from him.

"Oh," he breathed, eyes a silver fire that riddled her.

She shook her head.

"It's your grandfather's house," he said quietly.

She stepped back herself. Gramps would understand. Probably. She was well over twenty-one. He knew that she knew all about the birds and the bees. He'd known that she'd been married....

And he'd been longing to find the right someone to match her up with for ages.

But this was his house. And he might be back any minute. And it was simply a matter of...

Respect. The kind of thing that meant so very much to Jason Tarkenton.

A shudder ripped through her. No. She couldn't let him leave without touching him again. Without being held in his arms. Without creating another memory to hold fast to through the lonely nights that stretched ahead.

She knotted her fingers into her palms at her sides. She was not reaching out for him. She swung around. "I've a shower in my room. I'll see you downstairs." She indicated the pile of Brad's clothing. "I hope these things fit you. There's a one-hour cleaner in town. We can get your things back tonight."

"A cleaner?"

She shook her head. "A laundry."

She closed the bathroom door thoughtfully. It was good that he was going! They didn't even speak the same language; they just thought that they did.

Vickie hurried down the hallway to her bedroom and into her own bathroom. She stripped off her long dress and stepped blindly into the shower, jumping when a cold wall of water came down upon her.

The water was startling, cleansing.

It helped. A little.

Go back with him....

That was impossible. Absolutely. Blindly she found the soap. Mechanically she began to wash.

Impossible! He didn't understand, truly couldn't understand. This world had penicillin, pasteurized milk.

AIDS. Bombs that could kill a million people in one single explosion....

This world had Gramps in it, and that was all that mattered.

But maybe she could convince Jason to stay. Maybe Gramps had found some records. Maybe...

Maybe he could prove that John Tarkenton would live whether Jason went back or not. Could such a thing be?

She didn't know.

She stepped from the shower, toweling herself strenuously. She walked on into her bedroom, dug through her drawers and found soft old jeans and a pink knit shirt. She had barely crawled into the clothing when she heard something pelting against her window.

She walked to it, drawing back the drapes.

Jason was down there. She opened the window.

He had looked striking in his cavalry clothing, tall, commanding, assured.

Yet, in a way, he was more striking now. His tawny hair remained long and shaggy, just curling over the collar of the tailored shirt. The worn jeans hugged his form, trim hips, long hard legs. His hands were shoved into the pockets. The shirt was opened a button or two at his throat.

His eyes were alight, startlingly silver. And he was smiling. For once the incredible tension was gone. In the twilight below her, he could have easily been of her world, a part of it.

No, for the way that her heart leapt, it seemed that he was her world at the moment.

He smiled at her, his lips curling slowly, ruefully.

"I wouldn't feel right about the house," he said softly. "But I noticed a great barn out here. Clean, sweet-smelling hay. Good blankets."

She stared down at him blankly for a moment, wishing that she could freeze him there.

For all time.

"Well, all right," he continued, "maybe I'm being a little presumptuous. And then again…" He paused, and then his voice was deep and husky and passionate when he continued. "And then again, maybe I can't quite make myself care if I'm being presumptuous or not. There's the very good possibility that I might run back up the stairs and burst into your room. And carry you on out to see just how wonderful that old barn can be."

She inhaled sharply. Her knees were trembling. She closed her eyes for a moment. She should have been thinking that he was wearing Brad's clothes.

She had loved Brad so very much. She hadn't even managed a decent dinner with anyone else.

Until now.

And Brad, she thought, would be glad.

"Vickie!"

She moistened her lips.

He started to turn. "I'm coming up!" he warned her.

Her fingers gripped the windowsill. "No! No!"

He paused.

She smiled, biting into her lip. "I'm coming down!" she called softly, and spun quickly away to do so.

CHAPTER SIX

There were wonderful, incredible things to this new world.

None of them was more wonderful than Vickie.

Jason saw her slow smile at the window, and he saw her turn. He turned his eyes to the door of the old house—old by either of their standards—and he waited for her to emerge.

In seconds, she did so, the wealth of her hair streaming behind her, catching the last drops of sun, shimmering with red lights. She was wearing pants now, the same manner of pants he was wearing himself, and they hugged her hips, outlining with a fascinating clarity their curve and shape, the length of her legs, the subtle slimness and agility of her.

Hmm. So that was progress. People had ceased to wear as much clothing.

On Vickie, it *was* progress, he determined.

And as she approached him, he discovered again that everything else faded, the reality of a war that disappeared, the numbing incredulity that he had stepped into a different time. Everything faded for those precious moments, everything but the uniqueness of the woman.

In seconds she was before him with her stunning clear blue eyes and fire-lit wealth of soft auburn hair. He reached out to cup the cheek of the beautiful face and it felt as if all the desires within the universe burst forward within him. God, yes, she could make him forget the horror. Make him forget all he had left behind.

Because she was so important to him. With her courage, her fire, her determination. And with her simple beauty.

He groaned softly, then swept her up into his arms. Her fingers laced around his neck. Her eyes met his. Her brow rose delicately and the husky query in her voice sent hot shivers racing down his back.

"You don't mind barns, hmm?"

The sweet clean scent of her was intoxicating.

"Actually, ma'am, I'm mighty partial to barns."

Her lips curled in a slow, lazy smile. Keeping his eyes laced with hers, he walked the distance into the old red barn. He had happened upon the perfect place out there. A clean stall filled with fresh, newly mown hay. There had been an old blanket there, frayed but sweetly clean, too, and he'd cast it down already in very high hopes.

He carried her there and laid her down, taking her lips, marveling at the sweetness of them, of the giving that lay within her. The delicate pink tip of her tongue met with his, parried, rimmed his mouth with heady sensuality, met and locked with his once again. He wondered if he would ever understand what was so different and wonderful about this woman. He didn't think that it was time that had really changed her. From what he had seen so far, things changed, people didn't. He had been lonely and bitter for aeons, it seemed. Loving his wife, hating her death. In all those months nothing and no one had managed to dispel his deep sadness. It had been war, and survival and responsibility, he tried to tell himself.

But battle was not continuous—though it had seemed so at times. There had been nights in new cities, there had been women, lots of them. Women who made their trade with the soldiers, and women who had simply been left lonely too long, their men fighting the war, or lost to it. Often enough he found someone to ease those bitter fires of need that continued to rage in his body. But never someone who could touch his very soul. To change things. To change him.

Never...

'Til now.

And this was wrong, he tried to tell himself. He lifted his lips from hers, staring down at her as she looked back at him with beautiful, crystal-clear blue eyes, trusting eyes...sensual eyes. And damp, parted lips. It was wrong. Because he had to leave. No matter how wonderful this world was. He couldn't abandon his brother, and so he shouldn't be tarrying here. Maybe he couldn't find the way back through the darkness. Maybe he did have to stay the night.

He shouldn't be spending it here, with her, making the ties of silk and fire between them all the tighter.

Her fingers rimmed the length of his back, soft pressure bringing him back to her. Her lips touched his again. Melded with them.

He didn't care about the future or the past.

Only glorious present.

He felt her fingers pluck at the buttons of his shirt, then they were moving over his naked flesh. Something scalding burst and swept around him. He felt her touch like laps of flame as her fingertips and nails stroked over the expanse of him, through the short, crisp hair on his chest. Over his collarbone, lower, against the ribs, lower, near his waistline. The shirt was nearly freed from him already and he sat up, almost ripping it from his body. Those beautiful blue eyes of hers were still upon him, the rich length of her hair was spread out in the hay like a cloud around her head, still catching tiny rays of light to gleam reddish-gold. Her breathing was fast now, her breasts rising, rising and falling. He lifted her slightly into his arms, enough to discard the very soft shirt she had been wearing and discover another of her very fascinating undergarments. This one was all lace, a creation that covered, yet didn't cover at all. Beneath the sheer fabric, the dark crest of her nipple was clearly visible. Just the sight of it sent waves of desire cascading and crashing over him. He linked his arms behind her, supporting her back, and set his mouth upon her breast, teasing the flesh through the lace, touching it lightly, then closing his mouth upon it. She arched back with a little cry, fingers digging into his arms. In seconds he was frustrated with even that brief barrier of lace and he worked his fingers against the hook that held it there. The garment fell free. He crushed her nakedness to his and felt the wealth of searing warmth, the hardened peaks of her breasts pressed so sensually to the wall of his own bared flesh. They were upon their knees, their lips melding again. His fingers ran down the supple length of her back, caressed her spine. Then they moved to her flat stomach and found the button at the waistband of her jeans. Then the metal closure that went up and down...down, at the moment.

He pressed her back against the hay, working upon her jeans, tugging them down against the length of her body. They fell free. In the dim twilight she lay against the old frayed blanket in the hay with an incredibly seductive beauty, the underthings she wore upon her hips very like that which had covered her breasts, all lace, something that covered, yet something that didn't cover at all. He found himself reacting the same way. Having to touch her with the lace, against the lace, between the lace.

He met her eyes for one fascinated instant, then leaned low against her, his tongue rimming the band of the elusive garment where it lay just below her hips. The sweet fragrance of soap on her skin seemed to pervade him as his tongue first touched flesh and lace. Her flesh was ivory, soft, taut, fascinating. She moaned and writhed and whispered something as the wet fire of his tongue first touched against her. He worked it lower, tasting her flesh through those wisps of lace. Lace, and lower still. Her fingers fell against his shoulders, kneading there. His name fell from her lips like soft raindrops upon him, again and again. She whispered a "no," and he paused a moment. The exquisite shape of her lay against the hay, the beauty of her flesh, her slimness, her curves, the rise of her breasts. Her eyes were nearly closed, her head was tossing from side to side. He smiled and looked back to the lace. It had been the most sensuous stuff in the world. Now he was impatient with it, as well. He stripped it from her hips, down the shapely length of her legs. And he began to kiss and stroke her intimately again, sliding his tongue against secret places, feeling the writhe of her body grow wild and erotic, hearing her cries become reckless and gasped.

He rose above her but she came up with him, pressing against him once again, her lips burning hungrily into his shoulder, teeth grazing his flesh, fingers stroking erotically upon it. In seconds. Her lips found his, his throat, his collarbone, and then moved wildly down the length of his chest. He felt her fingers at his waistband.

At the metal thing that went up and down.

Down . . . now.

Her fingers were working against the material of his pants, shoving them low over his hips. Her hands curved over his buttocks and his breath caught while his heart thundered. Her hands moved and cupped around the bulging length of him and a hoarse cry tore from his own throat. He encircled her with his arms, lifting her chin, finding her lips. He kissed her with a hungry passion while she continued to stroke and caress him until he couldn't bear another moment of it. Pressing her back, he rid himself of the pants. Amazingly, he paused another brief moment, absorbing the beauty of the woman against the hay, the red glory of her hair, the perfection of her body.

All the wonder in those blue eyes that still gazed into his so openly and trustingly. He loved her face, loved the curve of her lips, the wonderful fire in her eyes.

His eyes fell. He loved so much more. The rise of her breasts, the curve of her hips.

A deep yearning groan escaped him. He was suddenly in agony; the pulse within him was so great. He rose over her, and then sank within her. Felt the feminine sheathing of her body, the sweet ecstasy of being inside her, one with her, knowing that his hunger would be eased. Their eyes met. He began to move and move. His arms wrapped around her. His lips found hers. Then nothing mattered but the movement, the beat the pulse, the hunger that increased in each tenfold, and then, again. She was liquid beneath him, liquid that molded, folded, met and matched his every thrust and need. He heard the sweet, crystalline cry that escaped her and shuddered deeply. A thrust again, and again, and he echoed the sound himself, raggedly, hoarsely, explosively. The world burst and shimmered. It had been so long. He didn't remember release like this, satisfaction so damned wonderful and sweet. He seemed to hold forever, loath to leave her, but then he eased himself to her side and swept her protectively into his arms.

The world had gone absolutely mad. Yet how could he regret it?

Even if John lay dying somewhere? If he had died already?

He closed his eyes, tightening his arms around Vickie. But she rose up on an elbow, looking down at him. "What is it?"

He stroked her cheek, shaking his head. "You are magic," he told her softly.

She smiled, her lashes fell, and she met his gaze again. "Mmm. But I've lost you again already."

He lifted a hand in the shadows of the barn. "Guilt," he said softly. "I'm here, with you. It's as if I've touched heaven. And somewhere out there..."

"'Somewhere out there,'" she repeated. "War rages. And maybe there is nothing you can do. Maybe we're not supposed to travel through time or change history. But you're here. Through the violence of that dark tunnel. Perhaps you're supposed to be here. Maybe you're not supposed to go back—''

He groaned hard, sweeping her back into his arms, then pressing her against the hay, his leg cast upon her. Her eyes were very wide and defiant at that moment and he felt both the sweet ache of sorrow and a new rise of passion.

"How can we know what is *supposed* to be? How can we even believe what *is?*" He kissed her again, feverishly. Time itself was the rarity between them. He suddenly didn't want to waste it. "I can't even try to judge it, I don't dare think about it. I have to go back!"

She sounded as if she was choking. "You don't have to go back! The damned war will be lost without you, men will die without you, time will go on—"

"But it's not so simple, or so grand!" he whispered. "My brother is back there, and whether the war is won or lost, whether the future is changed, cannot matter. I can't see through God's eyes. All I know is that I gave my younger brother a promise, and that I could not live anywhere with my sanity if I did not keep it!"

"You could be trapped in that tunnel. Trapped forever."

"The tunnel is frightening. But I still have to face it. I still have to go back."

She fell silent, watching him. He thought that he saw the glint of tears in her eyes, and he kissed her. Her arms wrapped around him.

They were silent for a long while. Then she murmured to him, "Gramps will be back."

He nodded, pulling away from her. He stood, collecting their clothing from the various places where pieces had landed. He was loath to watch her dress. Time had given her to him. Time would soon snatch her away.

His fingers knotted into his palms. With all of his heart, he wished that he could forget time altogether. Forget the war, forget the blood, the death, and the heartache. Forget it all and just stay here. There must be endless new treasures to see in this new world, so many places to go, and they must be so easy to get to in those horseless carriages. Surely medicine had advanced, life had advanced—bathing had definitely advanced. He could just stay here. He'd been so damned determined he was going to be honorable in this new affair of his, and honorable still surely meant marrying the woman he loved. He had friends married to Northern wives. Some of them had run home, returned to their fathers. Still wed, they lived in different states. Many times, they were still in love, despite the war. Despite the distance.

Different states, not different times, he reminded himself. He was falling in love with her. He wanted to marry her. Sleep with her anywhere, including her grandfather's house. Make love to her on clean sheets, against the softness of a bed.

It would be so damned easy to stay!

His fingers tightened, his nails digging into the flesh of his palms. He couldn't stay. John was back there. John was waiting. With the first light he was going back. He had to.

But her back was to him then. She was just buttoning the pink shirt that draped so sensual against her shoulders. He dropped his hands gently upon her shoulders, drawing her back to him. He kissed the top of her head, and a rush of tension swept through him. He had to leave her. He couldn't really ask her to come with him, ask her to leave a world of hot dogs and Coca-Cola and come back to a time when the fury of war raged and blood ran hot between two sides of a warring nation. She couldn't come back; he couldn't ask her to, and he wouldn't want to endanger her.

But leaving her now was already like leaving a piece of his heart. The best of it.

She spun around in his arms. She saw the sorrow in his eyes. Luckily, perhaps, she misinterpreted it. She stroked his cheek tenderly, studying his eyes. "So much must hurt you!" she whispered. "And I'm so sorry. And honestly, Jason, I am a Virginian, I love Virginia, but more important, I'm an American, and you can't imagine how important that has come to be over the years! What's gone on between America and other nations since your time, you can't possibly imagine. There have been wars. Horrible, devastating wars, wars with bombs that kill tens of thousands of people at a single hit." She shook her head. "I'm so sorry for what you're suffering, but the North had to win. Had to. It was necessary for the United States to become the power that it did." She hesitated. "Jason, if you go back, you can't change things."

He caught her hands and kissed each of her palms. "Your grandfather was going to the library?"

She nodded.

"Can you take me there?"

She nodded again.

"Do we ride the horses?"

She smiled and shook her head. "I have something called a Jeep Cherokee out back. It will be much less noticeable parked at the library," she assured him.

She took his hand and led him back around the barn to the drive where her bright red little Cherokee waited. The key was under the mat and she opened her door, found it and slid into the driver's seat, indicating that Jason should sit next to her. He did, hands moving over the upholstery, eyes riveted upon the Jeep's panel. "What are all those?"

"Umm—that's for your speed, that tells you how much gas—fuel—you've got. Let's see ... windshield wipers, radio—"

"Radio?"

Vickie geared the car into life. She switched the knob for the radio and laughed when he stiffened like timber when the music blasted on.

He stared at her. "Airwaves. I think something like the telegraph probably led to all this," she explained.

He nodded. "It's loud."

"It can be turned down," she said, and did so. She started to drive. He stared straight ahead as she eased the car down the mountain, heading for the center of town. Luckily the night was quiet. There was almost no traffic. Everyone was either at his or her encampment or motel. Or maybe people were worn out from the day's activities.

Or resting for tomorrow's. The hardest fighting of the real battle had taken place that third day, and it would be the same with the reenacting.

Gramps was still there, she saw, as she parked in a space next to his old Buick. Jason stepped out of the car, looking at the buildings in the center of town.

Many of them were old, some even older than the days of the Civil War. But some of them were new. The newspaper building was sleekly made with glass panels everywhere. Very modern. Jason just stared at it. At that moment, she heard the distant rumble of a jet. She looked up as Jason did. His hands on his hips, he stared.

"Men have walked on the moon," he murmured wondrously.

"Well, those men—and women—are probably just flying from Washington to Memphis, or some like destination. That's an airplane, not a spaceship. Moon travel isn't commonplace. Although," she added thoughtfully, "they say that someday it might be."

"People can fly. They can just fly anywhere?"

"Almost anywhere."

Vickie watched him staring up at the sky, fascination in his handsome features. His hands were set upon his hips and she found herself watching them next, remembering the way that they felt against her, sensual, exciting, tender.

She was really, truly, falling in love with him. With his smile, with the flash of his eyes.

With the way that he made love.

And even with his determination to leave her. To go back.

She cleared her throat. "Let's go in. Maybe we can find out what Gramps is up to."

But as they started to walk into the library, Gramps was coming out. He seemed distracted and walked past Vickie without noticing her.

"Gramps?" she said, touching his arm.

"Vickie—Jason! What are you two doing out here?"

"Jason wanted to come to the library," Vickie said, frowning. "What's the matter with you?"

He had two very old books clutched in his hands. She saw that one was a history of Virginia companies of the Civil War, and another was an old, and probably out-of-print, history of Blackfield's Mountain.

Gramps looked at the two of them, shaking his head. Then he sighed. "Let's go somewhere. We can't just stand here in the doorway." He peered at Jason, who was watching him with a keen interest. "You still hungry, young fellow? We got a great steak place just yonder and it's late enough now not to be too busy."

"I'm still hungry, sir. But I still haven't any money—"

"Don't friends invite friends to dinner in your time, Jason Tarkenton?"

"Yes, of course."

"Well, I'm asking. And if you're any kind of gentleman, you're accepting."

Jason bowed his head slightly, hiding a smile. "Thank you. I accept your invitation with great pleasure. And I even know what a steak is!"

"Thought you might," Gramps said, and he grinned, but Vickie saw that the humor wasn't really touching his eyes. He was worried.

They didn't take the vehicles. Hunter's Place for Steaks was just up the road and they walked the distance in a few minutes. They were soon seated in one of the booths. The waitress asked them for a drink order. Jason hesitated, looking at Vickie.

"Have a whiskey," Gramps suggested. "I sure intend to."

Jason nodded. Vickie started to order iced tea, but watching her grandfather, she decided she could use something stronger herself and ordered a rum and Coke. Gramps asked Jason if he might just order for them all and Jason nodded politely. It was going to be a simple meal. Three T-bones, three baked potatoes and three great house Caesar salads. The waitress left them, and Vickie finally exploded, managing to do so in a whisper.

"Gramps, *what* is it?"

He sighed. He drummed his fingers on the table. Then his blue eyes set upon Jason and then her, and Jason again. "I thought I could find something in the books that would keep you from going back. For instance, maybe the history books would say you had just disappeared in the middle of the battle. And some brilliant doctor picked up your brother and he went on to live a long and happy life and survive the war and have a half-dozen children."

"But that's not what happened," Jason said evenly.

Gramps shook his head unhappily.

"Well, what does happen?" Jason demanded.

Gramps sighed. "Your brother, John, had been in the middle of some medical training before the war started, right?"

Jason nodded. Vickie gasped. "How could you know that?"

"Vickie, you should know. The military tends to keep pretty good records. Even though a lot of the stuff pertaining to the Confederacy was lost, you forget, the Daughters of the Confederacy and all those veterans' organizations were strong, even back then. This book was written by a Virginian war widow back in the 1890s. And it has a fair amount about a Colonel Tarkenton in it—and a John Tarkenton, too.''

''Gramps, *please,* get to the point!'' Vickie insisted.

He still stared at the two of them a long moment, with Jason returning his stare. Gramps was very old and wrinkled and bald; Jason was in his prime, his tawny hair thick and rich, his face lines clean and striking.

Still, somehow, they looked very much alike at that moment.

''Your troops do very well in the battle, Jason. You lose only three men, and two are reported missing. Neither of them is your brother. He's injured, but you get him to a field hospital and you stay with him. The surgeons want to take off his arm, but you don't let them. His arm heals.''

Jason's head was lowered. ''Thank God,'' he murmured.

He looked up. He realized that they were both staring at him, stricken.

''I always knew I had to go back!'' he told Vickie softly.

''There's more to it than that,'' Gramps said wearily. ''You save Lee's life right before Gettysburg, battling it out with a sniper before he can get to the general. Everything could change if Lee died.''

''Maybe I can save others now—''

Gramps leaned toward him, shaking his head. ''No,'' he said slowly. ''Don't you see? You can't try. You can't change history. You can't keep Stonewall alive, you can't risk changing the outcome of the war in any way."

"Then why the hell do you think this all happened?" Jason demanded suddenly, passionately. "Why should all this have happened, anyway? Maybe I *am supposed* to *change* the outcome. Maybe that's why I'm here—"

"No. You're here to save your brother."

Jason fell silent, staring at Gramps. "What do you mean? If I hadn't been away from him so long, I would have done much better saving him. I can only believe in you now because I'm so desperate to do so."

Gramps tapped his fork against the table, then looked at Jason again.

"There's a museum down in Petersburg. A pretty good little Civil War museum.... Anyway, the big battle at Petersburg is yet to come for you. It's pretty close to the end there. But I always remember, there's a little piece of sponge there. And there's a comment that some of the Confederate surgeons knew ahead of the Yanks that it was dangerous to use the same sponges on different men. We know now, of course, that germs were spread that way, that half of those men died of diseases because of those dirty sponges. They didn't really know that back then—they didn't understand all that we do now about germs and bacteria and viruses. That's the point."

"What point!" Vickie cried out.

Jason was staring at Gramps. "I think I've got it now, sir. You think that I'm here so that I can go back and save John—so that he can go onward and start men on their road to discovery. With his injury, he'll be sent home. And he'll start to practice medicine—"

"And he'll get others to start using clean sponges. And he'll save any number of lives," Gramps finished. "And his work will also start others on the road to discovery." He hesitated a moment, then continued. "Dr. John Tarkenton is behind some of the first research done in the field."

"Excuse me?"

They all turned. The waitress was there. "Drinks!" she said cheerfully.

Vickie didn't wait for hers to be served. She plucked it off the waitress's tray and took a deep swallow.

Her heart was pounding. *She had known. She had known he was going back. He had said it again and again. But maybe she had believed like Gramps that there might have been a way to make him stay!*

But they all knew it now. He had to go back. There was no hope. There were no choices.

Warm, strong fingers curled around Vickie's beneath the table. His eyes were on hers. Dark, silver, intense.

She was searching lamely for something to say when they suddenly heard a strangled gasp. Then there was the loud—and close!—retort of a shotgun blast. All three of them spun around, as did the other dozen or so patrons remaining at the restaurant.

A tall, scar-faced man in a dirty brown leather jacket stood at the register, with a shotgun leveled at the pretty blond cashier.

"Not another word!" he shouted out over the clientele. "Not a sound from one of you, or the idiot queen here—" he caught the girl behind the register by her hair, causing her to shriek again as he dragged her out before him "—gets it, ladies and gents, right in the head. Brains and blood all over your dinners, folks, so just stay still. Real still.''

They were still. Everyone in the restaurant.

Everyone but Jason. Vickie could feel the tension in his body.

She squeezed his fingers, sending him a silent message. *Don't!*

Then someone let out a terrified little gasp and the man spun around, throwing the pretty young cashier forward as he did so. She tripped, and he slapped her hard across the head. "I just came in because I needed a little quick cash. I didn't mean for anyone to get hurt, but I'll do whatever I have to. Understand me? Don't make me kill you, girlie.''

Vickie felt the horror constricting her throat. The girl didn't mean to be giving him any trouble—she was just so scared silly that she couldn't stand properly. He started to pull her and she fell again. He swung the shotgun around, ready to knock her across the temple with it. Vickie forgot that she had been willing Jason to silence. He was bounding up, but she barely noticed him because she hadn't been able to keep still herself. She had somehow heard an imaginary sound in the back of her head, a cracking sound, the sound they would have heard if the man had managed to send the butt of his shotgun crashing against the girl's head.

Victoria screamed out, "No!''

The man paused. The shotgun started to level at her. He shoved the blonde away. "No? Fine, then *you* can get over here and get the money out of the register.''

Everything happened so fast then. The blonde fell against the front counter. The thief crossed the few feet to their table and was reaching for Vickie. Gramps was up.

But Jason was behind her.

And before the man could close his fingers around her wrist, Jason was around her, flying at the thief, thrusting her far behind him, to safety.

He slammed against the man.

She heard the sharp retort of the gun once again. Jason and the thief fell hard to the floor together, rolling toward the front door of the restaurant.

She screamed, starting to leap for them, but Gramps was pulling her back. "Wait, Vickie, wait! Let me see—"

"No, no!"

He was moving! Jason was moving. Straddled over the thug, Jason delivered a solid punch to the man's left cheek, and then the right. In the center of the floor, in front of the sobbing cashier, the robber was stone-cold unconscious and Jason was trying to scramble to his feet.

Vickie heard the scream of a siren.

Then she heard a burst of applause. The men, the women, the children, all the people in the restaurant, the clients, the help, everyone was clapping.

Jason turned around, smiling sheepishly. His eyes immediately sought out Vickie. He started to walk toward her. "That awful screeching sound means that the law is on the way, right?"

"Right—" she started to say.

But even as she spoke, he suddenly pitched forward, falling against her.

Blood stained the tailored shirt she had given him to wear. It seeped onto her pink knit, into her hands as she clasped him.

"Gramps!" she shrieked.

And then Jason's weight dragged her down to the floor. She cradled his head against her, smoothing back his bloodied hair.

She cried out his name, and then began to sob it.

Over, and over, and over again.

CHAPTER SEVEN

The waiting was a nightmare.

They wouldn't let her in, not once the ambulance reached the hospital.

Then, of course, there was that horror that probably would have been as shocking to Jason as the stark white hospital walls and the emergency room staff and the heart monitor and everything else—

Paperwork. Jason might well be astounded to realize that people just didn't let you into hospitals anymore, not without insurance, not without pages and pages of information.

She and Gramps just stared at each other at first, then he nudged his leg against hers. "You've got the card, Vickie. Give the nice lady the card."

Vickie just stared at him for a moment. She was feeling so horribly numb to begin with. She felt like bursting into tears, like melting into the floor. He had left a war, to be shot in an armed-robbery attempt.

It didn't seem just.

She had fallen in love with him.

And now she was losing him. Not because of the wicked violence of the tunnel, or the war. Because of *her* world.

She was going to lose him no matter what.

Not this way.

"The card, Victoria!"

The only insurance card she had was in Brad's name. She'd never bothered to change the name. "Give the lady Brad's card, Vickie, come on now."

She drew the card out of her wallet and handed it to the emergency room clerk. The woman was being very patient, and understanding.

"That's fine," the woman said. "I'll just take all the information off this and return it to you in the waiting room over there. I'm sure the doctor will be right out."

There were cops crawling around then, too. There were a few minutes when the waiting was broken up by the questions that were fired her way. They were easy to answer. The whole thing had happened in just a matter of minutes. She just had to remember to keep calling Jason Brad, just in case someone from inside the hospital was listening. And then she had to hope that no one she knew came in at that moment, and blew the whole thing. She'd given them Brad's card, so it was assumed now that she was Jason's wife.

"How are we ever going to get out of this?" she asked Gramps.

He shrugged. "Does it matter? As long as we got him admitted?"

She shook her head. She still felt so numb. Then a man clad in white walked out into the waiting room, obviously looking for someone.

She gasped, recognizing the man.

He was very tall and ebony black, a handsome man with striking, strong features. His height had always compelled attention.

He certainly had Vickie's card now.

She'd never gone on to medical school, but she and Sam Dooley had taken a number of courses together in their very first year of college. She had known that he had gone on staff here, but had just forgotten about it completely.

Now, of course, his eyes found her. And he stared at her hard. "Vickie. May I speak with you now?"

She leapt up and stared at Gramps. He started to rise, to come with her.

No, whatever it was, she could handle it, she could handle it. And maybe Gramps couldn't....

"I'm all right!" she promised quickly.

She rushed over to Sam Dooley. He nodded gravely to her grandfather, opening a door that led into a hallway with doors on either side.

He leaned back against a wall, a chart in his hands, suspicion in his eyes.

"Vickie," he said softly. Then, "Just what is going on here?"

She shook her head, her lips very dry. "Sam, how *is* he? Please, how is he? Oh, my God, he's not—"

"He's fine."

"He's what?"

"He's fine. The bullet grazed his head, nothing more. There was a ton of blood because of where it struck. Of course, there's always the danger of concussion, but really, he could probably walk right out of here tonight. I think it's better that he stay for observation, so I'm keeping him. But you can see him."

She started to turn, seeking a direction in which to go. Sam clamped a heavy hand down on her shoulder.

"Who is he, Vickie? He isn't Brad Ahearn, I know that."

She inhaled swiftly. "I had to use Brad's card—"

"To get him in here. I understand that."

"He's just a friend. I really don't—I don't know a great deal about his past. But I do know that he's a good man. He probably saved that little cashier's life. Sam, please, I wish I could explain—"

"It's like he walked out of another world."

"*What?*" Vickie gasped.

Sam kept watching her very curiously. "Well, for one, at first he kept asking me for the real doctor. I told him I was the real doctor. Then he looked right at me and exclaimed, 'A *darkie* is a real doctor?' Well, now, Vickie, I always have been bright enough to know that I'm a black man, but in all my days, no one has ever called me a *darkie* before. Now, more than that, Vickie. The man in there is scarred. As if he'd been hit with something like a saber a number of times! Now, you put that with the way that he's talking, and gawking at everything, and you have one strange man!"

She stared at him blankly for a minute. "Sam, he—he was just shot in the head. He's probably not feeling quite right."

"Hmm... Is that it? Vickie, who is he really?"

She sighed. "If I told you, Sam, you wouldn't believe me."

"Try me."

Oh, yes. Try him. She bit into her lower lip. She met his dark gaze. "He's a real Civil War soldier, Sam. He stumbled into our world by some strange connection through time. Gramps seems to think that the reenactment has something to do with it.''

She got the exact response she had expected—sheer incredulity. He stared at her, speechless at last.

"I told you that you wouldn't believe me."

"Have you told this to anyone else?" he said dryly.

"Just my grandfather."

Sam threw his hands up. "I give up!"

She caught his hand, holding it as she stared up at him imploringly. "Sam, please, I'm begging, keep quiet about him. He's going to have enough difficulty dealing with the police, with the media. Please—"

"He's not some kind of fugitive or criminal, is he, Vickie? That's not why he's been all cut up, is it?"

"No!" she cried quickly. "Sam, I swear to you, he's a good man. Please, just keep quiet. I beg you."

"I'm not sure it's ethical."

She shook her head wildly. "Sam! He saved a life. On my honor, I swear he's no criminal."

"He just stepped out of the Civil War to check out the reenactments, right? Is that it?"

"Sam—"

He freed his hand from her grasp and wagged a finger under her nose. "All right, Vickie. I won't say a word. For all I know, he might be another Brad Ahearn. I'll keep quiet—just so long as you get your fellow in there to quit calling me *'boy.'* That's what he went to after *'darkie.'*" He threw his hands up in the air again. "Eight years of school, two years in a residency. And all I get is *'boy'*!"

"*Dr.* Dooley, I think you're wonderful!" She gave him a quick kiss on the cheek. "I'll get him into line. I promise. Where is he?"

"Upstairs. Room 306. You better go quick and tell him what his name is supposed to be. The police want to question him."

Vickie thanked him again and fled to the elevator. In seconds, she was hurrying down a hallway to his room. Jason was sitting up in bed, hair tousled, eyes a bit wild, clad in a washed-out hospital gown. There was a bandage against his left temple, but nothing more.

"What is this damn thing?" he asked her irritably, plucking at the material of the gown. "There's no back to it! I feel . . . naked!"

She smiled. He was fine. He was really fine. She hurried to him and threw her arms around him, kissing him warmly. She drew away, arms still around him. "It's a hospital gown. And you have to wear it or else really be naked until I get a chance to run home and get you something else. Oh, God, Jason! You're all right!"

He heard the trembling in her voice and took her very tenderly into his arms again. "I'm fine. Just fine. I'm sorry you had such a scare. I must have blacked out just a shade there. But it's just a scratch. I've been injured much worse before."

She'd known that. She'd seen all the scars that had awakened Sam Dooley's keen interest.

"You saved my life," she told him.

"I don't know if your life was ever at risk."

"He meant to take me with him."

"Well, I'm not sure what it means these days, but he was certainly no gentleman."

She smiled. "There really are gentlemen these days, still. My husband was one. Steve, the man you met, is full of honor and caring and all kinds of great things. But there are men like the one you brought down, too.''

He stroked her cheek. "There always have been."

There was a knock on the door. "Oh!" She said quickly, "Listen, I had to use my husband's old insurance card to get you in here."

"What?"

"Never mind, I'll explain later. They only give you medical attention free these days if you're actually killed, and then the coroner gets his shot at cutting up your body. That's cynical, isn't it?"

"I don't know what you're talking about."

"Right, I know, and I don't have time to explain. Just remember, when they question you, you need to say that your name is Brad Ahearn. Just while you're here, all right?"

"What?"

"Brad Ahearn," she repeated. The knocking was more insistent. What could have been an absolutely horrible incident had been averted. The awful man could have held a restaurant full of tourists hostage. Or worse. He could have started shooting. As it happened, Jason had managed to subdue it all. The police had been handed over a downed perpetrator, everyone else had gone away alive and well and unscathed—except for the terrified blond cashier, and she had been tranquilized right on the scene—and now Jason was even proving to be alive and barely scratched in the hospital.

The police surely wanted to close things up. All they had to do was get a statement from Jason now.

They wouldn't knock politely much longer.

"What's your name?" she hissed to him.

He shrugged, shaking his head. "Brad Ahearn? If that's what you want."

She started to walk away to open the door to his hospital room, then she hurried back to him. "And be careful, will you? We almost had a real problem. I went to school with Sam Dooley, and he's a great guy and a great doctor, but he was also on the football team and if you call him *'boy'* one more time, he just might come out swinging!"

Jason winced and grinned. "I had forgotten," he said quickly. "The Yanks win, right? Slavery is abolished. Imagine! Well, you're right, Vick. He seems like a darned good doctor, too. I'll watch my words."

She swung around quickly, reaching the door just as it opened. The two officers waiting impatiently there were from the county. She was relieved to see that she didn't know either of them.

Officers Hewlett and Macy looked a bit like clones of one another, both about an even six feet, dark haired, lean faced and in county gray uniforms. They addressed Jason as Mr. Ahearn, and never questioned his name.

"You came in from the Staunton area for the battle, sir, is that right?"

Jason stared at Vickie, a brow arched, a smile curving his lips.

"Yes, that's right. Darned right," he said.

Officer Hewlett asked him to describe what had happened in the restaurant. Jason did. The officers took notes, but it appeared that everything was in perfect order.

"Well, sir, we're mighty glad that you did come over for this one. You might have saved some lives tonight. The fellow holding up the place came out of a prison called Raiford, in Florida. He's been making his way north over the bodies of a few unwary travelers. I don't think he would have thought twice about killing a hostage in this situation. Not twice. You've done us quite a service."

Jason shrugged. "Me, or someone else. The restaurant was crowded. Too many of us there for him to think he could just corral us all. Someone would have stopped him."

The officers looked at each other. They definitely thought that Jason wasn't quite all there. Sane men didn't risk their lives.

"Well, I think that that's all we need for now," Macy said. He then added politely, "The doc said that you might be wanting to get a little sleep now. We'll need to get hold of you again, of course, but I believe we've gotten your address—it's the one you gave us downstairs, right, ma'am?"

Vickie nodded, swallowing quickly.

Hewlett and Macy started for the door. She walked along with them, ready to close it in their wake. Hewlett paused, looking back to Jason.

"That's quite an incredible man you got there, Mrs. Ahearn."

"He's not my—" she started to say. She bit off the words. Well, Jason was supposed to be Mr. Ahearn here in the hospital. But that wasn't what made her pause.

"Yes, I do have an incredible man there," she assured Hewlett, smiling. *Truly, you don't know the half of it! He's quite incredible,* she wanted to add.

She closed the door behind the officers firmly, and turned back to Jason. He was watching her, smiling. He slipped from the bed, then seemed to realize that the back of his nightgown was open all the way down. He tried to draw it together as he approached her. He couldn't quite grasp the sides of it.

"Oh, the hell with it!" he murmured, taking her into his arms. His lips touched hers. "That's awful language to use around a lady."

She smiled up at him. "I've heard it before. I've used it rather frequently, I'm afraid."

He smiled, and kissed her again. "I have to get out of here," he told her then softly.

She shook her head. "You might have suffered a concussion. They don't want to let you out."

He arched a brow, frowning. "I've gone back into battle with just a bandage around broken ribs. And they want me to stay in here because of a cut on my forehead? Vickie, you know I've got to get out."

She pressed him back toward the bed. "Jason, you can't just go waltzing out of here. And it's still the middle of the night. You have to wait until morning. Doctors make their rounds very early. I'm sure they'll release you right after sunrise."

The door opened then, without a knock sounding. A nurse was walking in with a tray. There was a syringe on it and a little white paper cup of pills.

Jason stared at her, remembered his open hospital gown, and started grabbing for edges again, backing toward the bed. He stared at Vickie reproachfully, with warning eyes, as if she had allowed someone entry here when he was so ridiculously vulnerable.

She smiled. She couldn't help it.

The nurse, a slim, attractive brunette of about thirty, looked from Jason to Vickie with a little sigh that seemed to say, "Guys! Great big he-men types, but you show them a little needle and they just go to pieces."

"Hello, Mrs. Ahearn, Mr. Ahearn. My name is Sheila. Dr. Dooley has ordered a tetanus shot for you since you didn't seem to know when you last had one. He hasn't had one recently, has he, Mrs. Ahearn?"

Vickie smiled at Jason. "Not recently. I'm sure he needs one. I'm absolutely sure of it."

Jason's eyes narrowed her way.

"Come now, Mr. Ahearn, you need the shot," Sheila told him cheerfully. She walked around the bed, setting her tray down on his nightstand and flicking the needle carefully. She stared at Jason. "You need to roll over please, Mr. Ahearn."

"I need to what?" he demanded.

"Roll over, Mr. Ahearn. A tetanus shot is very important—you must know that, Mr. Ahearn. It protects you from infection."

"You need the shot, you need to roll over," Vickie stated.

"If I need the shot, you had best find another place to deliver it!" Jason insisted. "I'm not rolling over for any female nurse—"

"Mr. Ahearn!" Sheila protested, her eyes wide. "If you can't behave, I'm going to have to call for the doctor—"

"I'm not rolling over—"

"Yes, you are!" Vickie insisted. She caught his hands. He stared at her. Hard. As if he was going to really strangle her the minute he could get his hands on her. She smiled sweetly. "It's necessary. It's very customary. Brad, it keeps you from getting an infection. It's good. It lasts a long time!"

"He doesn't know about a tetanus shot?" Sheila said curiously.

"You know men," Vickie said, staring hard at Jason. She reached for his hand. His fingers curled hard around hers.

"It's not going to hurt."

"It's not pain that I mind."

He gritted his teeth. He returned her stare with a hard violence in his eyes.

"Mrs. Ahearn, really, can you give me a hand with your husband? I have to have some cooperation! If not—"

"Brad, shift over. *Please, my love!*"

He shifted. Still holding her hand. Still staring at her.

"That's good, I can get you from there!" Sheila assured him. She bathed a spot of flesh with an alcohol swab and quickly gave him the shot. Jason didn't blink. He kept staring at Vickie.

Sheila made a *tsk*ing sound. "It's a good thing God didn't decide to let them have the babies."

Vickie quickly lowered her eyes. Jason's fingers squeezed hers, but Nurse Sheila was moving around between the two of them with the little paper cup of pills in her hands. "These will help you sleep."

"They'll what?" Jason said suspiciously.

"Honestly!" she said, shaking her head to Vickie once again. "You've had a rather hectic evening, Mr. Ahearn. Just in case you have difficulty, these will help you sleep. Come on now, Mr. Ahearn."

Vickie thought that he took the pills. He crumpled the little paper cup in his hands and accepted the glass of water Sheila poured for him.

"All down now," Sheila said, flashing them a bright smile. "Mrs. Ahearn, that chair stretches out into a cot, if you want to stay with your husband. If you need anything, just hit the nurses' call button. Anything at all." She hesitated a minute. "It was a pleasure to meet you, Mr. Ahearn. That was quite a brave thing you did."

"Anyone would have done it," Jason said flatly. He felt Vickie's gaze. "But thank you," he added quickly.

Vickie smiled and followed Sheila to the door. "Don't forget, just press the call button if you need anything. Oh, my—I almost forgot. Your grandfather is still waiting downstairs, Mrs. Ahearn. We've assured him, of course, that Mr. Ahearn is going to be just fine. But he's waiting to have a few words with you, whenever you get a chance."

"Thank you. Thank you very much."

"Good night, Mrs. Ahearn. Call if you need me."

"Thank you. I will. Good night."

She closed the door, and started to walk slowly back to Jason. He seemed to be staring straight ahead of himself. He didn't even seem to realize that she was coming near.

Then he started suddenly and turned back to her. She remembered the way that he had stared at her when he'd gotten his shot, and she hesitated.

"Come here!" he growled.

"Not when you talk to me like that!" she protested.

"All right," he drawled broadly, stretching out sideways on the bed, supported by an elbow, "Come here, *my love,* my dear little wife!"

"Did you want to get into the hospital or not?" she demanded. "And you were terribly rude to the nurse. Now I know that you had women nurses in your hospitals, even if the idea of women acting in such a capacity was rather new!"

"She was walking around just as if she owned the place. As if she had the right to tell me what to do!"

"Nurses rather do in a hospital. Most of the time, they're nice and polite because their patients act like adults."

He made a snorting sound. "Women all over," he muttered. "Next thing you know, they'll have the vote!"

Vickie smiled knowingly, deciding that she would enlighten him when he wasn't so riled up.

"An educated black man for a doctor!" he mused.

Vickie took a step closer to him. "Do you own slaves?" she asked him softly.

He looked at her for a moment without speaking. Then he nodded. "But I'm going to free them when I go home," he told her softly. "Not because I know now that the war is lost. But because I've met you."

"Not to mention Dr. Dooley," she reminded him softly.

"Who seems a very fine man."

Vickie smiled. He leaned forward on his elbow, moving closer to where she was standing and, as she bent down, his lips brushed hers very tenderly. Well, at least he wasn't going anywhere tonight. And maybe the tetanus shot he'd had here would help him when he—when he went home.

She didn't have much longer with him, she thought, and the pain seemed to tear into her. Just tonight. And he was in a hospital bed, doped out, ready to sleep.

It didn't matter. She'd stay with him. At his side.

"This whole place is pretty amazing," he told her. "So very clean. So quiet, so well organized. The machines—the shots. Medicine has come an incredibly long way."

She inhaled and exhaled slowly. "Yes, that's true. But we've new diseases, too. Killer diseases. We've managed to do away with the old, but we've been deviled by the new."

"Imagine, though. A tetanus shot. Something that protects against infection." He rolled over suddenly, reaching out to her. "That's what John needs. That— and a clean sponge, like your grandfather was saying. If I could just get him one of these shots, I could keep him from getting gangrene."

Vickie nodded. "Maybe," she murmured. He didn't seem to notice that she was there again for a moment. "Well, we can talk about it in the morning. Those pills you took will make you drowsy very soon," she told him. "I'm not going anywhere, though. I'll be here with you. Gramps is still downstairs. I just want to say good-night to him so that he'll go on home, okay?"

Jason nodded. "Tell him thank you for me, will you?"

"You'll see him again."

He nodded. His answer took a minute to come. "Tell him thank you for me, anyway."

"I'll be right back," Vickie promised.

She hurried down in the elevator. Gramps was standing in the waiting room. Her heart surged out to him. Of all the strange things she had done to him over the years, this had to be the strangest!

Bringing home a time traveler, and expecting him to cope!

But Gramps did. Magnificently. Gramps always did.

"Gramps?"

He turned, tall and straight for all his great age, his blue eyes sharp.

"He's really all right?"

"Just fine. Ornery as all hell, but just fine!" Vickie assured him with a grin. "They'll probably release him in the morning. Can you bring us both some new clothes? These things have blood all over them."

"Sure thing. You're going to stay with him here, I take it?"

Vickie nodded. "Do you mind?"

He lifted her chin. "Victoria, I wouldn't expect any less from you, granddaughter. That's one of the reasons I love you so much."

"Gramps . . ."

"The other is that, of course, you look like me. Well, not now, but when I was young and good-looking."

She grinned. "Go home and get some sleep."

He nodded, but he still paused. "It's a shame, Vickie. A darned shame. Hold him a little bit longer.

Then you're going to have to let him go. You know that."

"I know that."

Gramps left and she went back up in the elevator, wondering if Jason might have fallen asleep already.

But he was awake, sitting up in bed, flicking the channels on the television. He stared at the screen, then shook his head at her.

"There are so many amazing things!"

"I imagine," she said softly.

He patted the bed beside him. She hesitated, and then came over. His arm came around her, his lips brushed her forehead.

"Good movie?" she asked him.

"I don't know, but I'd like to see it with you. I'd like to do so many things with you."

She smiled. "Making love in a bed would be nice."

"The nicest."

"I'm going to get into the chair so that you can sleep—"

"I don't need to sleep."

"But the pills—"

"These?" He lifted the paper cup, crumpled up with the pills still inside it.

"Yes, those!" she said with flat reproach.

"I may need them later," he said softly.

"Nurse Sheila could come back."

"Let her," he said softly. "I just need . . . to hold you. That's all."

She eased her head down on his shoulder. She needed to be held. To feel his arms around her. To know the tenderness, and the caring. It was all such a wonderful feeling.

The comfort and security were so sweet that her eyes began to close. She nudged against him more closely.

"I love you, Vickie," she heard.

She tried to open her eyes. *I love you, Vickie.*

They were such wonderful words.

Her lips curled into a slow and wistful smile. "I love you, too, Jason. So very much."

"I will love you forever," he told her. "Forever."

His fingers smoothed over her hair.

It was the last thing she remembered. She slept deeply, dreamlessly, surrounded, encompassed, by feelings of comfort and warmth and tenderness. . . .

But then she was curiously cold.

"Mrs. Ahearn?"

She awoke to find a nurse staring at her. Another nurse. A heavyset, buxom woman who looked very confused.

"I'm sorry, Mrs. Ahearn, but I understand your husband is the patient. Isn't he supposed to be in the bed?"

Vickie jumped up. She stared at the bed. She had grown cold, of course, because she had been alone.

Jason was gone.

The bathroom!

She tore into it. Jason wasn't there. He was gone.

"Mrs. Ahearn?" the nurse said, concerned.

Vickie spun around. He was gone. Really gone.

She looked out the window. It was first light.

And then she knew.

Yes, he was gone. Really gone. He hadn't wanted to say goodbye, but he had headed for the mountain.

"Mrs. Ahearn?" the nurse said again.

But Vickie didn't hear her. She was already running out of the room.

She didn't know what she was going to do herself. She only knew that she had to catch up to him before he reached his doorway to the past.

CHAPTER EIGHT

When Vickie first left the hospital, she was at a loss.

She had left her Jeep at the library, having ridden the few minutes to the hospital with Jason in the ambulance.

Now she needed a cab, and they weren't that common in this kind of a small town.

"Damn!" she cried out, her heart sinking. Then she saw a green Volvo pulling out from the doctors' lot. It was Sam driving.

"Sam!" she cried, running in front of him. He slammed on his brakes, then leaned his long frame out of the window. "Vickie, have you lost your mind completely? I might have killed you!"

"Sam, can you get me home? I know you've been on a long shift, I know how tired you are, but I have to get home quickly!"

"Is your grandfather all right?"

"Oh, yes, he's fine. I think. I just have to get home."

He stared at her, but leaned back into the car, pushing the passenger's door open. Vickie ran around and slid into the car.

Sam started to drive. She leaned back, closing her eyes. She felt him watching her, but she didn't know what to say.

"So where is my patient?" Sam demanded.

Her eyes sprang open and she stared at him.

"I imagine he's taken off, and that's why you're in such a hurry to get somewhere," Sam said. "Your house?"

She bit her lip, shaking her head. "No, I don't think that he's still there."

"But he went there?"

"Well, he needed his horse and his uniform—"

She broke off, realizing that Sam was watching her.

"His sword, his gun? His men? Are they all running around your house, too?"

"Sam, this is serious!"

Sam sighed. "All right, how did he get to your house?"

She shook her head. "I don't know. Oh, I know that you don't believe me, but you can just quit making fun of me, Sam Dooley."

"Vickie, have you considered that he may be a madman?" he asked her worriedly.

Vickie smiled, looking to her lap. "I thought of it. I thought of it a lot. But he isn't. He isn't mad at all. He's just rare—very, very rare. As rare as Brad!" she said softly.

Sam sighed. At that hour, they hadn't hit much traffic, and in just a matter of minutes, he was pulling up to her grandfather's driveway.

"Thank you, Sam. Thank you so much," she told him.

She started to open the door. He caught it for a moment, and met her eyes. "This just may tie into something, Vickie. Early this morning one of the nurses in Emergency was preparing a tetanus shot for one of those reenactors who had cut himself up on his own bayonet." He paused, and Vickie arched a brow to him. "The syringe disappeared, all ready to go."

"Oh," she said softly.

"Vickie, will you pay attention to me? He could be dangerous."

She shook her head. "You don't understand. He needs it. His brother was wounded up on the mountain."

"Then he should bring him to the hospital."

"I don't think that he can." She leaned over and kissed his cheek impulsively. "Thank you for the ride. And for everything. Sam, you know that I'm not crazy, and I swear to God, I'm telling you the truth!"

Sam sighed, sitting back. "I don't know where this man is going to lead you, Vickie!"

"It doesn't really matter," she said. "I—"

"You what?"

"I'm in love with him. I never thought that I could love anyone again."

"Vickie—"

"Sam, I've got to go. I have to find him. I can't just let him disappear without saying goodbye."

Sam let her go. Vickie ran up to the house, calling for Gramps. He burst out onto the porch just as she reached it.

"I tried to call you at the hospital, Vickie. But you'd run out just as I got through," Gramps said.

"So he was here? He came here?"

Gramps nodded. "Came back for Max, his uniform, his sword. I tried to hold him. He said that it was too hard to leave you as it was. Told me that he loved you." He hesitated a minute. "Told me that he'd love you through all time."

"Oh! How did he get here? How long ago did he leave?"

"Seems he managed to hitch a ride easy enough, down the highway. Walked the rest of the way. He's only been gone a few minutes. I've got the horses saddled out back."

"You've got the what?"

"The horses saddled. Your Arabesque and old Dundee."

He suddenly tossed her something. It was a clean white blouse. "Your shirt's got bloodstains on it. Come on, let's go."

He was out the door while Vickie was still struggling into the clean shirt. She followed him quickly enough. "Gramps! What do you think you're doing? You—you can't come with me. This ride is too hard—"

"Am I still living and breathing and in my own senses, Victoria?" he demanded.

"Living and breathing, yes, but I was never too certain that you were in your right senses!"

"Young lady, you keep at it and you'll get your mouth washed out with soap."

"Indeed?" Vickie said, but she was panting then to keep up with him.

"Do you think I'd let you go alone, Vickie?"

She shook her head. "Go? Gramps, I'm not *going*. I wouldn't leave you. I just have to—"

"To what?"

"To say goodbye. To tell him to come back if there's ever a way. To tell him—"

"That you love him, too."

She nodded.

He wagged a finger at her suddenly. "Don't you ever give anything up for me, Victoria Ahearn! Ever. I'm an old man. Not much time left."

"Don't you talk like that! I'd never leave you—" she started to say, and she knew that that was exactly what she was afraid of. "Gramps, it never, never occurred to me to go back! To a life without cars, without washing machines—my God, I'm still a young woman. I could conceivably have a half-dozen children. Could you imagine having to go back to a life without disposable diapers?" She smiled brilliantly for him. "Gramps, go home!"

He swung around to her. "Not a chance, Victoria. You listen! I've studied it, my whole life! The Civil War. I've collected, I've lectured, I've sold. I'm taking you to that doorway, Vickie, and that's that!"

She sighed and threw up her hands.

"Besides," he said smugly, "I actually know the mountain much better than you do. I know the exact places where all the skirmishing took place. Can you say that much?"

"I know them well enough."

"Well, do we stand here arguing like stupid old asses, or do we ride?"

Vickie walked on past her grandfather, leaping up on Arabesque. He was one stubborn old coot.

And for all his years, he could still swing up easily enough on old Dundee. They started out, Vickie leading the way.

They came through the back, past the area where the reenactments had already taken place, where the landscape was still heavily trampled and an occasional paper cup still lay around. Then she hesitated, trying to remember where she had been. She pictured the place past the Yankee encampments where Jason had first accosted her. Then she tried to recall where it seemed they had traveled back in time for those few brief moments.

"May I?" Gramps drawled.

She swung back in her saddle, looking at him. He rode on past her, spurring old Dundee into a canter.

"You're going to have a heart attack!" she called to him, giving Arabesque free rein to catch up.

But it was the best she had seen Gramps look in years. He grinned back at her. "Who wants to live forever?"

She shook her head, riding hard beside him. And amazingly, it seemed that Gramps did know where to go. Vickie recognized all the terrain they covered. Even as they rode higher and higher.

The first indication that they had come to the right place was the sky.

Vickie reined in, feeling the hard gusts of wind swirling around her. "Gramps?" she murmured uneasily.

She looked up. The blue day had gone very gray suddenly. Dark clouds were massing above her, some of them nearly black. The wind picked up with a low, chilling moan. Gramps was near her. Old Dundee was backing up and prancing nervously. Beneath Vickie, Arabesque was doing the same thing, her hooves kicking up clumps of dirt and rock.

"There's sure as hell something going on out here! It's going to storm," Gramps cried. Then he looked at her, his eyes wide with amazement. "The wind is circling here like a cyclone! Feel it! It's not coming from the east or the west, it's circling!''

"I remember this!" she cried. *Yes, this was what it had been like. This was the area that surrounded the break, the doorway, in time.*

And she had *passed through it before!*

Yes, this was it, Vickie thought. They had come too late. Jason was gone. They had missed him.

She could hear the awful cry and whip of the wind. It seemed to be building. She tried to control Arabesque as she looked around the slope of the mountain. She reined in, her mouth feeling dry. Ahead of her, right ahead of her, barely visible against the darkness that had arisen around them, was an archway of trees. Huge, tall trees, old trees, nearly as old as time itself, bent over and arched into a perfect arbor. Hesitantly, she nudged Arabesque over to the opening of it. Her breath caught. There was movement. Far at the end of the archway, she could see shadowy movement. A horse! A horse and rider.

"Jason!" she cried his name.

But was it him? She couldn't tell. Whoever it was didn't seem to hear her. The rider didn't stop.

And sitting there, she began to feel the cold, clammy sensations of fear come creeping over her again. The place did exist; yes, it was real, it was a break in time, extraordinary, and not quite right. The wind wasn't right, the feel of it was more than odd—unearthly. She realized suddenly that in the tunnel, she wouldn't really be anywhere, not in her world, not in his, just captured in a dark swirling void between past and present.

She couldn't go forward. Couldn't feel those awful, clammy fingers of dark wind and chilly air touch down upon her, wrap around her.

She couldn't do it.... But if she didn't, she'd never see Jason again. She couldn't go through that dark, terrifying passageway. She had to go through.

She swung around, staring at Gramps. "Stay there! Just stay put! I'll be right back."

She nudged Arabesque hard with her heels then. The horse reared up, and she tightened her thighs to hold her seat. "Don't you dare go getting temperamental and overbred on me now, Arabesque. Don't you dare!"

Arabesque landed on all four hooves. Then she leapt forward, bunched her muscles and started to race.

As Vickie urged her horse forward, the wind whipped cruelly around them. She tried to rein in on the mare, crying out a "Whoa!" But Arabesque ignored her, snorting and galloping her way wildly into the swirling green-and-black darkness. Vickie lay low against her neck, wincing, clinging hard to the horse lest she be killed in the violence of the fall she would take if she lost her seat. God, it was awful! A wild, reckless gallop that she couldn't control. It was terrifying. She could feel some kind of walls. Walls, yes, invisible walls, tightening around her. Cold, clammy. Touching her.

Dear Lord, she thought! It was growing smaller! Changing. The door in time, if that was exactly what it was, was beginning to close.

Of course, she thought bleakly, the battles were almost over.

Air rushed and shrieked by her. Terror filled her. She kept riding. Hard. She closed her eyes against the blinding forces of the wind and Arabesque's whipping mane. Then she screamed out again for it seemed that the mare came to a halt just like a well-trained barrel-horse, right on a dime. Arabesque reared high again. Vickie still clung to her. The mare landed hard.

And the world seemed to explode.

There were men everywhere. Men mounted, men afoot. Shots were being fired, saber duels were taking place in front of her.

Bodies lay all about the field. Bodies in blue, and bodies in gray.

For a moment she stared, disbelieving, even after all that she had come to believe.

There were so many things to see.

The mountain had changed little. Men changed. The earth, if let be, did not. The terrain was still deep green and brown; it was littered with the yellow and purple of wildflowers. Trees and clumps of rock lay strewn about naturally as always.

Yet covered with fallen, bleeding men.

So many were so different. The Yanks seemed fairly uniform, but some of the Rebs were in kepis and some in slouch hats.

Some wore gray, and some wore faded, tattered colors that were no longer really discernible.

Some still fought, and some were in retreat. While Arabesque pranced and Vickie fought to control her, she could see that the fighting was going bad for the Rebs. In good order, they were forming a retreat up the mountain. They couldn't come down any farther, but they were going to hold their ground. They fought all the way.

Horses were rearing, screaming.

Men were screaming, crying out. The Yankees were taking the field before her. Oh, God! Had Jason come through? If so, where was he now? What could she do? Try to reach him?

Leave. Turn around and leave. There was nothing that she could do here. Gramps was behind her, waiting for her.

"Ho! You there!" someone called out.

She turned around. She blinked. There was a great deal of powder in the air, adding to the grayness of the day. The wind was still whipping it around, causing her eyes to sting.

There was a Yankee officer on a horse trotting toward her. She tensed, suddenly wondering just what she had done, and wondering now if she wasn't the mad one, not Jason.

She was in the midst of the war. The real one. It was incredible.

It was true.

"Who are you!" the man demanded. "State your business."

"I live on the mountain," she said. He still stared at her demandingly, a man of about forty with a beard and sideburns. "It's my home!" she told him.

A younger officer rode up behind him. A man with long blond curls and a slim face and watery blue eyes. "It's another one of those Southern spies, sir! Look at her, look at the way she's dressed, riding a horse like a man." He spit on the ground and Vickie gasped.

"Well, excuse me!" she cried furiously. "And just who the hell do you think you are? And what the hell do you think you're doing on my damned mountain!"

As soon as the words were out of her mouth, she realized her mistake.

Too late.

"Smart mouth on her, too. She's a Southern spy, I swear it, like that girl from Front Royal, Belle Boyd. Like that Mrs. Greenhow in Washington, the one who caused our boys to be mown down back at Manassas!"

"I'm not a spy. I'm just looking for someone!" she said.

"Who?"

"An officer. A—"

She broke off.

"A Reb!" the blond man proclaimed, as if he had caught her in the act of murder.

The older officer moved his horse closer to hers. "And just what is it that you intend to tell this man— this Reb—once you find him?"

"What could I tell him?" she asked with exasperation. "You've already met up with the Rebs, they know where you are, you know where they are! Just what could I possibly have spied upon that everyone involved here doesn't know already?"

"She's a clever one!" the blond man said.

The older man nodded slowly. "Maybe you know something about Rebel reinforcements. Something that could keep the Rebs fighting harder and longer."

"I don't know anything—" she said, then she broke off. Yes, she did. She knew everything that happened here. Jubal Early was due to bring his troops in at any time. Stonewall Jackson had sent for him, putting out a cry for help. And when Jubal Early made it, the Yanks were going to be pushed back. They would still claim victory; losses would be nearly equal, but the Rebels would keep their hold on this little piece of Virginia until the end of the war.

"Jesu!" the older man exclaimed. "She does know something!"

A third man rode up. He was older still, very weary looking, silver haired, sharp-eyed. "What's going on here, Lieutenant Granger?" he asked the dark-haired man.

"I'm afraid we've found a local spy, sir, trying to reach a certain Reb, Colonel Bickford."

The newcomer looked Vickie up and down with curiosity. "It's dangerous business, ma'am, stumbling around in the middle of a battlefield," he told her in a light tone that still carried a note of warning.

"I'm not a spy."

"She sure is!"

"You sure she's even a Reb?" the colonel asked.

"Ain't ever seen no Northern girl dressed like that," the nasty-tempered blond man said.

"That's enough from you, Captain Harper."

Vickie gave her attention to the colonel. "I'm not carrying secrets or messages. I'm just looking for a man to say goodbye."

"Your husband?" the colonel asked.

She hesitated a second too long.

"Not her husband!" the blond Captain Harper said, pouncing once again. He rode his horse slowly around Vickie. "Not her!" he exclaimed softly. "She wouldn't have time these days to settle down, to be a lady. Who are you looking for? A man, but not your husband. Someone to just fill a few of the hours that might be long and lonely otherwise? Well, ma'am, we've lots of Yank soldiers where we're going. Maybe you'll find another one you like."

"Captain Harper, that's enough!" the colonel insisted.

But Captain Harper had seemed to quickly acquire a deep and hostile interest in her. "We're not going to lose this battle, sir, because of a snooty Southern spy."

"No!" Vickie cried. "You're going to lose it because of Northern idiots like yourself who can barely sit a saddle!"

"And the Southerners are so much better, right?" he demanded, very close to her, a fanatic's sizzle in his eyes.

"You bet!" she promised softly. And the second that he came just a step closer, she nudged her heels hard against Arabesque's side.

Her mare leapt forward. She leaned low over the mare's neck, becoming one with the animal. She wasn't at all sure where she was going, just away. She couldn't go back to the archway in the trees; she couldn't even see it anymore, the settling of the powder had obliterated it. She started across the mountain, climbing, praying....

And wondering, too, if there was really anywhere for her to run.

It wasn't possible....

It was.

They were thundering after her. Arabesque was a fine mare, no matter what frame of comparison was made, against horses of any time. She could run like the wind.

And she was outrunning the nasty blond captain so set on Vickie being a spy. But even as she raced forward, there was a whistle and cry.

She was besting the men behind her.

But a string of ten riders was circling around her now, riding down, having given up on their pursuit of the retreating Rebs.

She reined back. She tried to seek out a route of escape.

There was none. She urged Arabesque to try to break through the ring of riders.

She had paused too long. The angry blond captain, Harper, had caught up with her. He threw himself from his own horse to hers, catching her from the animal, sending her hurtling to the ground with him atop her. A sense of panic seized her. She tried to struggle free from him and she knew that some of her punches caught hold of him good, but though he was slim, he was strong. He was quickly straddled over her, pinning her wrists to the ground. His eyes touched upon hers and chilled her. They were filled with both hatred—and lust.

He was a Union officer! There were now dozens of soldiers around. He couldn't possible hurt her, not really.

And he couldn't. Not then. The colonel came trotting up. "Captain Harper, I do believe that our prisoner is subdued. Let her up now, son."

"She's dangerous, sir, surely you saw that!"

"Tie her hands. Set her up on her horse and lead her back to camp."

Vickie stared at the colonel, clamping down on her jaw as her hands were wrenched forward and quickly tied with a red scarf someone supplied.

"I'm not a spy!" she told the colonel. "Call off this creature of yours!"

But despite her words, Captain Harper was lifting her and setting her upon Arabesque. His eyes really sizzled now. "Nice filly," he said, gazing into hers. "Good flanks. If you decide to look for a Yank this time instead of a Reb, I just might be available."

She spit at him. He stepped away neatly.

"Yep. Maybe I'll see you later," he told her, and then he grinned. "And then maybe I'll see you hang!"

He meant her, not the horse. She tried to kick him.

"Harper, get on your horse!" the colonel commanded. He reached for the reins to Arabesque. "Call in your company, Captain. I want an orderly formation back to camp!"

Wrists tied together, forced upon Arabesque, Vickie had no choice but to be led along. Chills started to race down her spine. The mountain looked the same! It was covered with grass, with trees, with wildflowers....

It wasn't the same at all. They broke through a section of forest and down an incline and there, in the valley, she could see the Yankee encampment. It seemed to stretch forever.

So many more tents than there were for a reenactment!

Huge tents, command tents. A-frame tents that stretched on and on forever....

And no hot-dog stands on the sidelines. None at all....

She bit her lip, fighting the chills. She closed her eyes, trying desperately to remember all the history Gramps had taught her over so many years.

The Yankees hadn't really hanged any female spies, had they? Rose Greenhow had died, but she had drowned when her ship had gone down, returning from Europe with gold for the Confederate cause.

Belle Boyd had lived a very long life, performing in the theater, lecturing, dying at an old age in the North.

Mrs. Surratt had been convicted of being part of the plot to assassinate Lincoln. She had been the first to be hanged, hadn't she?

The first that history had recorded.

But things had happened during the war that *didn't* make it into the history books. Innocent victims killed by stray fire. Rapes, plundering, robbery.

No...

She was going to be all right, she assured herself. The absolute worst thing that she would face was the lack of a proper bathroom.

Captain Harper was a son of a bitch in any age. But it seemed that the colonel was a decent man, and he was the one really in control. Surely he wouldn't let them hang her... would he?

She stared at the tents again. Soldiers were riding in—some were starting cooking fires, some carried around the wounded. Some were in full uniform, some in half dress. There were at least several regiments of the Union Army here. Old men, young men. Drummer boys who couldn't have been more than twelve. Graybeards who made Gramps look like a youngster.

And they all stopped now, stopped whatever they'd been doing. Stopped to stare at her as the colonel led

Arabesque on into the camp, heading for one of the large tents in the center of the field canvas.

They were were dead silent at first. Then someone cheered, and someone else waved. Vickie stared back, eyes wide.

Then a young fellow called out, "Pity we haven't a few like her on our side, eh, Colonel?"

"I'm sure we do, son, I'm sure we do!" the Colonel called back.

But I'm not a spy! Vickie longed to call back. *I'm just looking for a man!*

Her heart thundered. Jason. What was going to happen now? He didn't know that she was there, didn't know that she had followed him. Maybe he had found his brother. Maybe he had already injected him with the life-saving tetanus shot. Maybe he was carrying the wounded man to a field hospital.

Maybe all that had been done, and Jason had returned to his men, a bone-weary soldier who knew that he had to keep fighting, to do his best—and lose a war.

A deep, searing pain seized her along with a new sense of panic. She had lost Jason. And she had ridden into a nightmare. She had left Gramps behind. Waiting for her.

God, she had to escape. . . .

"Here we are, ma'am." The silver-haired colonel dismounted from his horse with the slow agility of a man who was accustomed to being in the saddle, and had grown tired of it, too. He reached up and plucked Vickie down from Arabesque. "What's your name, ma'am?" he asked her.

"Victoria Ahearn," she said.

"Well, now, Miz Ahearn," he said softly, "I'm sorry that I have to detain you, but I do. We don't know where the Rebel forces are around here, but I think that our rash young Captain Harper is right—you do know something. It's in your eyes. I'll have to keep you here until we move out. This is my command tent. There will be pickets around it, but you won't be disturbed. The general will make all the final decisions regarding you, but he's a good, decent man. When this is all over, I know that he'll let you go."

She shook her head slightly. She couldn't stay here while they battled away.

The passageway in the arbor of trees was growing tighter. She didn't know how long she had left to return before the passage closed—but it *would* close, she was certain. Every minute wasted in this camp put her return in graver jeopardy.

"Please, Colonel—" she began.

"Don't go wheedling me now!" he warned her. He reached for the tie on her wrists. "You better resign yourself to confinement. I truly wish you no harm."

Her wrists were free. She rubbed them, watching him still. What would he do if she told him that she didn't belong here at all, that the North was going to win the war, it didn't matter at all what messages she gave the South. Thousands and thousands more men were doomed to die; Lincoln was going to be assassinated—

God, no! They'd hang her for sure on grounds of treason if she even mentioned such a thing!

"Miz Ahearn, you get on in there now. I'll see that you're brought some water and something to eat, and we'll do our very best to see to your comfort, but make no mistake about it, you are our prisoner."

He turned away.

"Wait!" she cried out to him.

But the colonel was a busy man. He was already walking away. When Vickie would have followed, she was suddenly accosted by a uniformed man on either side, each catching one of her arms.

"If you will, please, ma'am," one of them said politely.

Vickie stared into his eyes. He was a young man. Achingly young. Probably not even eighteen.

"Please?" he said politely again. "None of us, none of us wants to hurt you, ma'am."

"But—" She fell silent, looking at him. Then her lashes lowered quickly. "Fine," she said, allowing her shoulders to slump.

Let them all think that she was resigned.

It might be her only hope.

She was led into the tent.

It was large, pleasant and spacious. There was a field desk in the center of it, a neatly made cot to the side, and several trunks piled up opposite from that. There were several chairs, obviously set up so that men could meet there and confer upon their strategy.

There was a bar set up next to the desk, too, she noticed.

There were glass flasks and silver tumblers.

All the niceties of home.

Oh, God.

The soldiers left her there, the young one smiling and assuring her they would see to her welfare. Vickie stared around herself, then sank down to the foot of the bed, covering her face with her hands.

She had to get out.

She was surrounded by tents, and those tents were filled with Yankees. Her enemies. No, they weren't her enemies! The war was over.

No, it was being fought right now.

She groaned aloud. Escape, she had to escape. Trick one of those handsome young boys somehow....

How? She fell against the colonel's neatly made cot. Her eyes filled with tears. There had to be a way to do it!

But time passed, and she lay there. Then she wiped away the dampness on her cheek. She would get nowhere lying there. She had to watch and listen. She had to be alert for her chance. The major battle should be today. Maybe the majority of the men would ride out. If she could just take advantage of the rise of confusion...

She strode over to the liquor flasks and found the bottle of whiskey. She wanted a shot, just one shot, for courage, to get her moving.

She poured it out into one of the silver cups. She tossed back her head and swallowed the liquor.

Then she heard a noise and she looked to the opening of the canvas tent.

Her heart seemed to shudder within her chest. Captain Harper was back.

Standing there, watching her, his hands rested on his hips and a slow smile curved his mouth. "Well, now," he said softly. "I wish I could join you. Can't, though, duty calls. But it's awful nice to know a shapely little spy like you likes both men and whiskey."

Vickie set the silver cup down, backing warily away from him.

"What are you doing here?" she demanded. "Shouldn't you be fighting Rebs? Maybe women are easier for you to best than taking on men your own size."

She saw the flash of anger that touched his eyes, but he kept smiling.

And he came closer. "I don't give a damn what you have to say, *Miz Ahearn*. In fact, keep it up and I'll gag you. I'll see that you can't have anything left to say to me at all."

"You'll gag me? The colonel—"

"The colonel is with the general now, trying to plot this battle. You see, you're not really too important around here. Not at all." He came closer, leaning against the tent post. "The lieutenant couldn't even come. Seems there are more Reb troops arriving, but then, you knew that, didn't you? What a shame. I'm all that's left. So I'll be moving you."

"Where?"

"Back to the main body of the army, down the eastern side of the mountains. Seems we can't quite let you go. We may even have to take you all the way to Washington with us."

"You can't do this to me—"

"Ah, but we can. This is war—ma'am," he said mockingly.

God, no! He couldn't take her away! She'd never get back.

"Wait, please—" she murmured, backing away still farther. "Wait—"

But he had caught her. His hands were on her wrists. "You can come with me riding on your own or tied over a mule. Which is it to be?"

She forced herself to remain dead still. "I'll come along on my own," she informed him icily. "You don't have to tie me up."

"I don't think I'll need to, either," he told her. He flipped open the tent's closure flap and she saw why. She was to have an escort of at least ten men. And it seemed that she was to be given one of the army's bay geldings. Arabesque was out there, but she was now wearing a United States Cavalry saddle.

"Can I help you up on old Billie over there? He's a fine horse. He has two gaits—slow and stop. You won't be running away this time, Miz Ahearn."

"I don't need your help," she said, walking by him.

But he caught her by the arm and she nearly cried out when he pulled her back to him. "Just remember, ma'am, I'm the man in charge here. And I think that little tarts like you don't much deserve to be treated like ladies. Do you understand yet? You're at my mercy. And I'm not a bountiful man!"

She jerked free of him, feeling panic race up and down her spine again.

Surely he still wouldn't dare hurt her. There were other men around!

Yes, but...

They were his men. And this was a war.

The bay was a big one. She hoped she could leap up without difficulty, especially the way that she was shaking now....

She managed to do so.

Captain Harper walked on out with a very pleased smile curved into his lips.

There was no hope for her. No hope, no hope.

Gramps came through shaking. He had forced his horse all the way, and he had forced himself, as well.

The feeling of fear was so intense coming into the arbor! Like nothing he had ever known before. Like being... touched. Grabbed. Like hands winding around him, taking hold of him, trying to...

Trying to hold on to him, maybe. Hold him back in a strange, dark, whirling funnel—damp, dank, green, chilling to the bone. Not here, and not there, not anywhere, really, nowhere at all.

He'd felt a strange tightening all the while, too. And he sensed that the door was closing. Not quickly. But inexorably. Bit by bit. Closing in, the winds twisting tighter and tighter. His horse had felt it. He had felt it. Whatever unknown power had opened this strange passageway had now decided to close it once more.

Some force—perhaps something in the stars, in the moon, in time, in magic—had caused the tunnel to open. Maybe the alignment of the planets and the sun. Maybe it was everything that had been so exact—the reenactments on the exact same days, the battles being fought in the exact places, even the temperature being just about exact—maybe all those things had caused it.

And now, all the planets and stars were shifting again. The battles and their mirror-image reruns were almost over. And so the gap in time would soon be closed.

He could quickly return the way he'd come—except that Vickie was here.

He couldn't leave her. Not when he didn't even know if she'd managed to find her Colonel Jason Tarkenton or not. There were just too many dangers here.

His heart was slamming. She was everything to him. He had to know she was safe. Then Gramps forgot about his granddaughter for a minute for he stepped out into the nineteenth century.

He reined in quickly, swallowing down hard at the horror of everything before him.

He'd fought in a war himself, the Great War, and so he knew a lot about it. He'd seen carnage before. But this was horrible. Men lay all about. Groaning.

Dying.

"Hurry up, there, eh!" someone shouted suddenly. Gramps quickly backed old Dundee against a tree so that he couldn't be seen. A Yankee orderly with a bloodstained apron was urging his helpers to rush some bleeding, broken bodies onto a wagon. "The Rebs will be coming back for their own."

A second orderly threw a body onto the wagon, wiped his hands down his front and nodded to the others. "Did you see the spy they picked up?" he asked, then whistled sharply. "We don't get many that pretty, eh, Willie?"

Willie snorted and laughed. "Sure don't. Fiery little thing she were, too, riding circles around that Cap'n Harper the way that she were. Too bad there were so many of them. She might have given him the slip."

"Yep, but if she had, we might be a-wailing in our own blood right now, my man. She's a spy, and a spy is a spy, no matter how good-looking!"

"What they gonna do with her?"

"Colonel wanted to give her to the general. But then all the bigwigs got caught up in their maps and calculations for the battle. She's been turned back to the cap'n to guard." The man sniggered. "They're supposed to get her down to the main army. But I'll bet you a gold dollar that pretty filly will never make it! The cap'n sure had his eye on her!"

Gramps realized that he was holding his breath and felt as if he'd probably explode in about another ten seconds. He exhaled, and looked down at his shaking old gnarled hands.

So this was what it had come to! How darned ironic. All his life he'd loved history, he'd longed to go back, to see it firsthand....

And now he was seeing it. And Vickie was at the mercy of some sadistic soldier.

He backed farther against a tree as another rider came rushing through, barely pausing.

"The Rebs are coming back. In force. We've got to clear out of here *now!*"

"Yessir!" Both men saluted. The rider went on.

"Hey, the Yank over there is still alive," the second one said. "Maybe we should—"

"Leave him! Unless you want to be a corpse yourself."

Both men hopped onto their wagon of dead, wounded and dying. The wagon began to lumber away.

Gramps edged old Dundee out from around the tree. He rode out into the field of fallen men, and when he looked down, he wanted to cry.

Well, this was the truth of it! This was authenticity!

He held still as a troop of gray-clad riders came bursting out onto the field. The leader saw him, called out, a hand in the air drawing the men behind him to a halt.

"Sir! Halt and identify yourself!" the young Reb officer demanded.

"I'm a Virginian," Gramps called out. "And a desperate one. I've got to find Colonel Tarkenton, out of Staunton, Virginia, cavalry. Can you help me?"

"Are you addled, old man? A battle is about to begin on this mountain any moment."

"I've got to find the colonel," Gramps insisted. "Is his company headed this way?"

Other men had drawn beside the officer. They looked from one to the other.

Then the officer looked back to Gramps. "Why are you looking for him?"

Gramps lifted his chin. It had to be good. He knew that it had to be good.

What the hell? He might as well go for the dramatic. He had to have their help. He loved Vickie, but there was no way he could rescue her from a Union Army escort by himself.

"My granddaughter's got some information for him. *Important* information. She, er, she learns things, you know what I mean? But the Yanks have gotten her. Colonel Tarkenton will move heaven and earth for this woman's safe return. I swear."

They would help him! Surely they would help him.

That was . . . if they could. If Jason Tarkenton had made it back. If he hadn't been shot down already.

"That's quite a tale, sir," the young officer said finally.

"Do you know Colonel Tarkenton?"

"He's my commanding officer, sir. He's at our command tent." The young officer paused. "I suppose I'd best take you to him now," he said finally.

Gramps grinned. Broadly. "Thank you, son."

He looked up at the heavens and whispered under his breath, "Dear Lord, this is mighty weird. Mighty, mighty weird. But I do thank you for the small favors!"

Then Gramps started to ride. And he grinned again. Darn, if he just weren't so awfully worried, this might be all right. He was actually riding with the Army of Northern Virginia.

If Liam could just see him now!

CHAPTER NINE

Jason leaned idly against the support of a gnarled old oak tree, trying hard to convince himself that the time he had spent with Vickie had been a fantastic dream, born from the simple confusion and horror of the war.

Maybe, in time, he would believe it had all been an illusion.

But it was awfully difficult to do at the moment.

Hurtling through the archway, he had landed right in the thick of battle again. Yet, in all the days that he had ridden and fought, he had never been quite so desperately determined to win, to break through, to escape the enemy, as he had just then.

He wouldn't die. He just wouldn't. He had come too far to fall prey to a Yankee saber before managing to return to John with help—and the tetanus shot he had stolen from the hospital. He winced a little at the thought. In all his life, he had never stolen anything.

But it was so insignificant when it meant saving John's life.

Well, he hadn't died. And he had found his brother. A company of his men had already stumbled upon him and carried him off the field. But John had insisted on waiting for his brother before being taken in to any field hospital. And so Jason had managed to return, slicing his way through the raging battle, to rejoin his troops in time to be with John, in time to slip the shot into him, in time to reach the field hospital and stand there like a furious mother hen, making damned sure that the surgeons used a clean sponge when sopping up his brother's wound. He wouldn't allow them to amputate, and he gave them a firm warning that they needed to use clean sponges on other men, too.

Most of the bone-weary surgeons merely stared at him, and Jason smiled, and surely looked like a madman. They just didn't know yet that they were spreading germs and killing men. If he tried to tell them how he knew, they would see that he was locked up somewhere, in a home for Confederate officers who had gone daft.

He left one of his privates, one of John's best friends, to stand guard overnight with his brother. But when he had last seen John, he had been sleeping peacefully, on his way to recovery.

Very peacefully. John would get in a full night of restful sleep. Jason had managed to get him to swallow the two little sleeping pills he had saved in the scrunched-up paper cup.

He brother was going to live.

And he was grateful, so damned grateful.

But at this moment, he wasn't so sure he cared if he himself lived or died.

No, he told himself firmly, *he wasn't the kind of coward to be so willing to die! He was going to fight the war, survive the war, hold on to end the war.*

It was just that he felt so damned weary and lost at this moment. He shouldn't feel that way, of course. Despite the carnage, he should be very glad for the small favors of life. His men had loyally cared for his brother. They had searched for Jason. They had readily believed that he had become separated from them by the battle, that he had climbed the mountain continually trying to get back to John. They believed him without question.

And they were ready to follow him again.

The action seemed to have reached a lull for the day, he thought. His men had been ordered back. Rebs and Yanks both had gone to retrieve their dead and wounded. The Yanks were worried about the Confederate strength, while the Confederates kept them guessing as they awaited reinforcements. Stonewall Jackson had directed General Jubal Early and his army to join them. Their troops, combined with Early's men, would push the Yanks on down the mountain and back north again. Hopefully....

He closed his eyes. They were going to take this battle. Hadn't Vickie told him so? Did it really matter? They were going to lose the war.

It was terrible to know too much.

And terrible not to care at the moment.

He would lead his men again. He would see it all out. At the moment, he was glad of the fleeting interlude of peace.

He hurt.

No saber wound, no grazing bullet, had ever hurt quite like this. Even losing his wife had been different. His grief had been swift, searing and painful, but somehow easier to accept. To understand. God had taken her. She was completely, irrevocably lost.

Time had taken Vickie. Time, and his own foolish sense of honor. No, it hadn't been foolish to love his brother. Hadn't Gramps said that he had to return and save John? John's knowledge would lead to medical breakthroughs in the future.

Now... now! He could go back.

But Gramps had also said that he was supposed to save Lee's life at some later date.

And that might be all-important, too. It might have something to do with the binding up of the nation. He couldn't turn his back on such a fate.

He could only remember how she had felt beside him, remember the blue beauty of her eyes, the openness within them. Remember her courage, her determination, her independence, her laughter. Her anger, her passion. The way it had felt to make love to her.

She existed, she lived. And he had only to turn his back on whatever responsibilities lay in this world and return to hers. An incredible new world.

He'd hardly touched that world. There were so many places she might have taken him, so many things he might have seen and done.

Did it matter? No, none of those things mattered. Cars or horses, old values, new inventions. People mattered. One person, who provided a reason to live.

And had he really been living at all since Lydia died? Until he had crossed that unique barrier, and come upon Vickie Ahearn? She had given him back his life. Could he really go on here without her?

Anguish tore at him. The door was closing. The strange passageway he had stumbled upon was closing. He felt the peculiar barriers of it as he had come through, almost like a swirling funnel, twisting tighter and tighter. In a short time—maybe by now—it would be impossible to move from this one world to the next.

"Colonel!"

He looked up, startled from his thoughts. Lieutenant Nigel Keefe was returning from a scouting mission with the rest of Company B. He'd scarcely been out an hour, but then, the last of the skirmishing had barely ended, and Company B might well be in need of a few minutes' respite. But they were excellent men, battle-hardened men. The cavalry had always been the eyes and ears of any army. His men were accustomed to finding the enemy positions, and then joining in the action once the infantry and artillery were advised. They'd ridden tired before.

Something unusual must have happened to bring them back.

Keefe was coming in fast, his horse foaming, prancing, shaking off bits of sweat to glitter in the now-dropping sun.

Jason stiffened, eyes narrowing, as he saw that they had been joined by an unusual horseman.

It was Gramps. Riding an ancient old horse, looking a little peaked and scared, but as curious as all hell, too, as he stared out at everything around him with his shrewd blue eyes.

"Colonel!"

Nigel Keefe leapt down from his horse before it had come to a stop. "We found him right at the scene of some of the fighting, sir. He asked for you right off. Seems some woman was trying to bring you information, but the Yanks got her."

Jason's heart slammed like a cannonball against his chest. For a moment, he couldn't breathe. "*Some* woman," Keefe had said.

"Do you know the old man, sir?" Keefe demanded. "He swore to us you'd back up his story."

"Yes, yes! I know him."

Jason stepped forward, hurrying to Gramps's horse, looking up at the old man. "What's happened?" he demanded quickly. "What are you doing *here?*"

Gramps looked up at the men all around them, then back down to Jason with a look that clearly said he couldn't tell him everything. "She came looking for you. She was supposed to be right back. I followed her. I heard some of the Yanks who were picking up their wounded talking about how they had picked up a spy. They have her under guard and are taking her down to the main army camp."

Jason backed away from Gramps, stunned. He closed his eyes quickly, stiffening, looking down to the ground, trying not to let his men see how close he was to losing control.

He looked up. "Lieutenant Keefe, you're in charge here again." He pointed a finger at Gramps. "You! Sir! You stay here, in my tent. Out of the way, and out of trouble."

"I'm coming with you!" Gramps insisted.

"That horse would slow us down—"

"Then I'll take another horse."

"You can't—"

"I have to!" Gramps insisted. *"Please!"*

Jason sighed with exasperation. He looked at the men in Company B, then turned and called over his shoulder. "Sergeant Morrison!"

"Yessir!" His staff sergeant, in charge of his personal welfare, came running out from the field of tents, saluting quickly.

"I need you to find something this gentleman can wear," Jason told him. "Anything that resembles a uniform. And borrow someone's mount. A good horse, one that moves like lightning."

"Right, sir!" the officer said, saluting.

"A uniform?" Gramps said.

"We're going into the enemy lines," Jason said quietly. "They'll hang you for a spy if you aren't dressed in some uniform, and if you're with us, sir, you're a Reb at the moment."

Gramps's crinkled old face lit into a smile. He saluted sharply and leapt down from his old horse with a surprising agility. He quickly followed the staff sergeant toward the tents.

"Lieutenant Keefe," Jason said, "I'll need to hear everything you know about enemy positions." He looked out over the men of Company B again. There were eighteen of them. Their captain, Jim Hodges, had been killed some time back. Hodges hadn't been replaced. The men fought under Lieutenant Keefe, with First Sergeant Jack Johnson often giving the orders when it came down to gritty hand-to-hand combat. Every one of the men in the company had been with him since he had first commanded troops at Manassas. He could trust them now when he needed them so desperately.

But he couldn't order them into this mission.

"I know you've had a rough time of it here up on Blackfield's Mountain," he told them. "You deserve some rest, for there's sure to be more fighting. I'm riding out to find someone who helped me survive. None of you is beholden. I need volunteers, and that's what I want, volunteers only. Drop on out if you want to sit this one out.''

Not a soul moved.

''We're going right into the enemy camp,'' he reminded them. And he looked around at a sea of stubborn faces. Jack Johnson, a square-jawed Irishman, probably somewhere around thirty years old. The Jenson twins, Stan and Ben, early twenties, blond, blue-eyed, quick to sing at night, never faltering in a fray. They were coming with him. They were all coming with him.

He looked down, wincing. He knew now that he had to stay. Even if he could find Vickie, wrest her from the Yanks and bring her to safety, she would pass back into her own world. He had to stay. It did go beyond his brother. *Somehow, he just wasn't really allowed to leave!*

''Thank you,'' Jason told the men quietly. ''Lieutenant Keefe, let's take a quick look at the maps—'' he began, but someone cleared his throat behind him.

It was Gramps.

And actually, he looked darned good in the Rebel cavalry garb. Tall, straight as an arrow. Very dignified.

''You don't need to look at the maps. I know where all the positions are.''

''He can't possibly know more—'' Keefe began.

''But he does,'' Jason said with a slow smile. ''This is his mountain, you see. He knows it backward and forward.''

''The mountain, maybe. But what about the Yanks?''

"He's been studying their—er—battle tactics for years," Jason assured him. "Lieutenant, I put my faith in him. You wait here for word about our next movement. If I'm not back, you'll lead the troops into battle again."

Moments later, Jason's horse, Max, was brought before him. He quickly mounted and looked over Company B—and Gramps. "Gentlemen, we ride in stealth. We've got to discover where she's been taken. And then we've got to discover just how in hell we're going to take her back!"

He lifted a hand and lowered it. And they began to ride.

Captain Harper didn't seem to be in any hurry to get her wherever they were going. The lowering afternoon sun was still beating down upon them as they left the gigantic field of Yankee tents behind, following a curving path farther down the rolling fields, heading for the depths of the valley.

They walked; they plodded along. She, Harper and an escort of ten men.

They had been riding for over an hour, weaving in and out through heavily treed trails and open fields, when Harper suddenly called a halt. "We'll rest here, men. There's a stream down through the foliage there." Vickie stayed on her horse, staring at him as he dismounted. Harper looked at her, smiling. Then he addressed one of his men, a tall, heavyset fellow with small dark eyes. "Sergeant Rieger, keep a lookout! A good one. Shout at the first sign of movement, shoot anyone who hasn't got a right to be here."

"You—" he pointed at Vickie, his lips curving into a deep smile "—you come with me."

"No," she told him quickly, her heart beating hard. His men were at ease, dismounting from their horses. But surely they wouldn't all let him drag her off!

"You can come down," he warned her softly, blue eyes narrowed with warning, "or I can come up and get you."

"No!" she insisted.

Then she cried out sharply because he meant it. His hands were reaching for her, dragging her down. She punched, slapped and scratched at him, screaming, protesting.

"Captain!"

One of his men cried out to him in dismay. She had been right! The Yanks were like any other men, some of them good, and some of them—like Harper—not so good.

But Harper knew how to handle the situation. He wrenched Vickie on down to the ground, his arm around her throat in a chokehold. She could barely breathe. He swung around and stared at the young soldier who had protested. "How can you forget Manassas?" he demanded. "The Rebs beat us back like a pack of fools—*and all because of a spy like this one!* Josh Miller, you hush up now. Your very own brother was slaughtered down in the valley because a *lady* spy like this warned the Rebs we were coming. How can you all be such fools! I took her, and I'm going to see that she pays!"

"But, sir!" the young solder exclaimed unhappily. "How will we explain what . . . happened?"

"She tried to escape, soldier. She tried to escape."

Harper whirled around with her. She gasped for air and feared she was going to faint. Her heart was pounding all the more fiercely.

Dear God, she realized with a growing, paralyzing panic, he meant to kill her! Rape her, kill her. He'd have to kill her, or she would tell everyone what he had done. He meant to have his revenge against her. So far in this war, the Rebs had sent the Yanks into retreat one time too many. Harper had been humiliated.

And there was surely no way to explain to this man that the Yankees were going to win the war, that the Rebs were going to be vanquished!

Captain Harper, she thought, wasn't just somewhat of a bad man. He was a lunatic, a fanatic.

And no matter how she fought and struggled, he was taking her away.

Away from his men, from the eyes of the world.

Down the cliff, and toward the water.

Gramps knew his business. He led them through the trails to a break in the forest that stood just above the valley field with its endless ripple of Yankee canvas.

They reined, he stopping his men effortlessly with a lift of his hand. They stood silent upon the crest, watching the activity in the camp.

A cry suddenly rose on the air, loud enough to carry across the distance.

Jason bit into his lower lip. There was a Yankee hospital tent down there. The surgeons were busy seeing to their wounded, doing what they could to patch up their injured before transporting them to hospitals in Washington.

There was movement down there. Men cleaning their weapons, tending horses, trying to relax, still ready. They all knew the troops would be meeting again.

The camps weren't so different. Not at all. Boys were writing to their mothers. Men were writing to their wives. None of them knew if it would be his last communication home.

He couldn't think about the Yanks now; he couldn't even think about the war now.

They had Vickie.

"What do you think?" Jack Johnson asked him, gnawing slowly on a blade of grass as they stared down at the activity together.

Jason looked to Gramps. His face looked very old and haggard now. He had gotten them there, all right. But now he was staring down at the Yankee camp with dismay.

He just hadn't realized how many of them there would be.

Jason pointed across the field to another clump of trees. "They've got to have a sentry there."

Jack Johnson nodded, hazel eyes grave. "You and me?" he said to Jason.

"I can go it alone."

"Better two."

"Maybe," Jason agreed with a rueful grin.

He turned around, addressing the others. "Jack and I are going to take the left field over there."

His troops nodded with understanding. They would remain where they were, just like a pack of sentinels.

"What are you doing?" Gramps asked him anxiously.

"We're going to try to get our hands on one of their pickets."

"But they won't give her back because we've got one of their men—"

"The plan, sir, is to have the picket tell us where Vickie is," he said softly. "If they've brought in a woman, I can guarantee you every fellow in that camp knows it now."

"But—" Gramps began.

Jason raised a brow to him. Gramps fell silent, then said quietly, "It's your war, boy. You know what you're doing."

His war, his enemy.

And they had *his* woman.

"Jack," Jason said, indicating it was time they moved. He nudged Max, and headed off, Jack Johnson coming along behind him.

They were good horsemen. And they were Virginians, accustomed to the terrain here. They circled around the summits, keeping a careful eye to the valley and watching their distance. They had come to the group of trees surrounding the east side of the camp. Jason signaled to Jack to dismount, and they both did so, leaving their horses then to circle around into the foliage from separate directions, treading silently upon the soft ground.

Jason saw the Yankee picket first. The man had probably been there a long time; it might have been the end of his duty. He looked very tired, and very bored. Jason was glad. It made him an easy mark.

Jason waited a moment anyway, watching him cautiously. The man took a twenty-yard walk, his rifle over his shoulder. He stretched, looked about and yawned.

Then Jason was glad he had waited because he watched the Yank pull a mirror from his jacket and signal back to someone down in the camp below. The flashes of light were returned to him.

An *all-clear* sign had been given.

Jason saw that Jack had come around, too, and was hunkered down across the small clearing from him. He nodded to him, motioning that he would move in first.

They waited, both tensed.

Then the picket turned his back on Jason, and Jason leapt out of the bushes. He sprang at the man's back, catching him in a throathold from behind before he even knew something was about to hit him.

Jack sprang forward, smiling to the picket, placing a knife warningly at his throat.

"We need some help, Yank," Jason warned from behind. He eased up a bit on his hold.

The Yank spit, but he was young and scared.

"I ain't no traitor. I ain't helping no Rebs."

"Then you're going die," Jason assured him. "Say a prayer, if you would, son."

He nodded. Jack came at the man more menacingly with his knife.

"Now wait a minute!" the Yank said quickly. "What is it you want, Reb?"

Jason smiled behind his back. Jack eased up with the knife. "Want to hand your rifle over, boy?"

The Yank did so quickly, with Jason's arm still locked around his throat.

"We're looking for a woman," Jason said softly.

The Yank hesitated a minute. Jason tightened his hold again and Jack set the blade against his throat.

"You're too late."

"Too late!" Jason exclaimed.

The Yank really thought that he was going to die. "She's gone—she's gone!" he yelped quickly. "Captain Harper is taking her on down to the main camp. He rode out about an hour ago. He—*hey!*"

Jason had him lifted off his feet, whirling him around to face the clump of brush where they had left the horses.

"Sorry, boy, you're coming with us," Jason said.

"I sure as bejesus am not—"

"You can come with us alive, or we can leave you here with your throat slit."

"A ride sounds fine," the Yank said quickly. "A ride sounds mighty fine!"

With his arm around her throat, Harper lifted Vickie cleanly off the ground. She tried to kick and struggled but he was dragging her quickly through the trees and the brush. There was a stream just below them. She could hear the gentle rippling of the water, the soft cry of the birds. As Harper dragged her through the foliage, though, she could see little except a blur of green.

And then he suddenly stopped, throwing her down.

She landed hard, but she landed on soft earth. They were right by the water, and the bank here was sponging and covered with soft mosses. The trees were closing in all around them, but as she tried to rise, she saw that the sun was breaking through upon the water.

Harper stared down at her, his hands on his hips. She had never seen such hatred in any man's eyes.

"You're making a mistake. I'm not what you think!" she cried suddenly, fiercely.

Those eyes narrowed. "I know what you are. Your kind have killed more men than bullets!" he swore.

She tried to rise, desperate to get away from him. She had nearly found her footing when his hand crashed savagely against her face, sending her reeling back down again. He pounced, straddling over her. He leaned low, trying to capture her lips.

She bit him and kicked him with all her strength at the same time. He bellowed out in pain, easing back, clutching his mouth and crotch.

But his weight upon her legs still pinned her down.

She tried to twist to escape from beneath him, a wealth of tears springing to her eyes while terror ravaged her heart.

Gramps...

He would think that she had just left him.

And Jason...

He would never know. Never know that she had tried to touch him, just one more time.

She would just die here, up on this mountain. Almost a hundred years before she had been destined to be born upon it.

"Bitch!" Harper shrieked. He caught her arm, wrenched her back. He rose up on his knees, his fingers knotting into a fist, his arm pulled back, ready to strike. If he hit her with such violence, she would lose consciousness.

And nothing else would matter....

"Captain!"

A warning shriek gave him pause. He stared upward through the foliage, toward the spot where they had left his men and the horses.

His man, the heavyset Rieger, burst through the greenness and stared down at them.

"Rebels coming, Captain! Coming fast."

Harper was up instantly. "Rebs! How many?"

"Fifteen, eighteen, I'm not sure. But they're riding on us fast."

Suddenly they all heard a cry. It was wild, a sound that seemed to tear up the air and the day. It was a cry of wild, reckless courage and danger. A Rebel cry, high, tearing through the air.

"Get up!" Harper cried, dragging her to her feet suddenly. He wrenched her against him. "And when I do get a hold of you, *ma'am*, you will rue the day you and your Rebel lover were born, you hear? Jesu, lady, you will pay!"

"No!" Vickie promised. "You will pay!"

He caught her arm, wrenching her around, dragging her up the rugged terrain he had just dragged her down.

They reached the Yanks and the restless horses. Harper threw her up upon her mount with a violence. Then he leapt atop his own, and they heard the cry again, wild, violent . . . closer.

And then Vickie saw them herself. Perhaps twenty men on wonderful, powerful mounts. Men in gray and butternut, in ragged apparel, elegant nonetheless. They rode hard, one with their horses, handsome in their fluid movement.

Jason was at the forefront. Jason, his sword held high even as he rode, the silver catching the glint of the sun, shining with vengeance.

Behind them, there were others. Gramps! Gramps in a gray uniform. Gramps, with a sword waving, too.

It was incredible. Absolutely incredible. But, perhaps, no more incredible than anything else that had happened.

The cavalry was coming.

Coming to her rescue.

Gramps!

And Jason.

Dear God, Jason . . . !

CHAPTER TEN

"Get her moving!" Captain Harper cried furiously. Mounted, he brought his horse, Arabesque, around behind Vickie's, his eye on the surging force of Confederates.

"You plan to outrun them?" Sergeant Rieger demanded incredulously.

"They've come for the woman!" Harper called quickly to his men. "She's going to give them all our positions, she's going to see that they know their own reinforcements are coming. We've got to get her away. Or kill her!"

"Jesu, Captain Harper!" one of the men gasped.

"Let's run her out, then!" another man cried.

"Make for those rocks, yonder!" Harper ordered. "We'll shoot them down as they come, damn now, courage men!"

He smacked Vickie's horse on the rump and even then, the old boy barely moved. Vickie tugged on the reins quickly, trying to get the horse to hightail it toward the raging Confederates.

But Harper was too quick, and too determined. He had Arabesque turned around and cutting her off before she could move more than ten feet.

"You'll die first, I swear it!" Harper promised her heatedly. "It's a pity I didn't get to taste what this damned fool Reb is ready to die for!"

"You're the fool!" she promised him. "You—" But she was cut off. Harper wasn't going to be caught out in the open. She tried to strike at him, tried to fight him. But in a matter of seconds, he had lifted her from the tired old horse and over Arabesque's saddle, throwing her facedown over the horse's neck. Then he slammed the reins against Arabesque's haunches and the mare took flight, racing ahead of the Yankee troops.

Vickie thought that she would die before they reached the rocks, that she would go flying from the horse's neck to the ground, and be pummeled to death beneath the pounding hooves. It seemed forever that she was slammed about there, tasting the mare's salty coat. Then Arabesque was reined in hard, and Harper was dragging her off the horse again.

"Take cover!" Harper commanded his men. "Take cover!"

They all fell back behind the rocks. Vickie shook off Harper for a moment and ran. In seconds, he was pelting down upon her, slamming her hard against the earth. His evil leer rose above her. "You'll never escape me, you little witch, I swear it!" She was wrenched up again and over his shoulder. She kicked and beat against him and he swore furiously.

But he didn't release his hold.

He dragged her down beside him behind one of the rocks for a moment, and she watched with him as the Rebels advanced. She managed to forget Harper for a single moment as she saw the two men she loved most in life, tearing up grass and earth, riding like God's vengeance upon these men. Her heart swelled with pride for Gramps, and with a certain awe for Jason—

he was magnificent; a horseman, a soldier, in his element now, calling his commands to his troops.

"Ready!" Harper called, and she realized that his men were loading their rifles, ripping open catridges, ramming balls down their barrels. They weren't repeaters, she thought fleetingly. These men, at least, weren't armed with repeaters. Not yet.

"Aim!" Harper cried.

"No!" she shrieked out, terrified of the volley of death that would follow.

"Fire!" Harper commanded.

The volley sounded, tearing apart the air. Vickie screamed again, her head ringing, certain that the world itself had exploded.

But the men were still coming. They hadn't missed a beat. In beautiful, elegant formation, they were coming. Then, even as she flattened against the rock, they were there, the Rebs, their horses' hooves sailing over the rocks, engaging in hard hand-to-hand combat with the Yanks.

For a moment, there were men everywhere, swords flying, fists swinging.

She saw Jason, just ten feet from her. He had dismounted from Max, and he was fighting a Yankee, their swords flashing. The tip of Jason's sword gleamed red with blood.

"Jason!" she shrieked.

He paused for a heartbeat. His eyes met hers.

"Watch out!" she cried, and in just seconds, he parried the man who had sprung at him. Vickie gasped with relief, then screamed as fingers suddenly and violently wrenched into her hair.

"Move!" Harper commanded her.

She braced herself against the pain and whirled, nails ripping down his cheek. He swore, howling out with pain.

But he was a determined man. He didn't lose his grasp. With his free hand he wrenched a knife from the sheath at his ankle and set it against her throat.

"Move!" he repeated.

And then she had no choice.

In minutes they were crashing through trees and bushes. She was blinded by dirt and branches and leaves. She gasped, coughing, struggling for breath. She tried to halt. Harper dragged her down.

Then, finally, they came to the water again. Harper paused, looked around. He gasped himself, pushing her away from him, doubling over to draw in air.

He turned his head toward her, smiling. "We've done it, *lady*. We've done it."

She shook her head. "You've done nothing!" she gasped out at him.

He stood slowly, smiling. "They're fairly evenly matched. Only a few men will survive to come for you. And they'll be searching this forest from now until eternity."

Vickie took a step away from him. "You know," she told him, "eventually, your own kind are going to hang you."

"It won't be until long after I'm done with you," he assured her. Then his blond brow arched and his smile deepened. "You must be something, for a troop of men to come after you. Even *gallant* Southern men. Cavaliers. You could live, you know. You could show me what you've got that's so special, lady. Maybe I'd be in such bliss, I'd be willing to die for you, too."

Vickie shook her head slowly. "I'd rather die."

His smile faded, his lean features went hard. "Fine. I'll help myself to what I want. And leave the rest for vultures!"

He lunged at her.

"No!" Vickie grated out, sidestepping to escape him. She did so and he teetered precariously on a rock for a moment. She turned to flee, praying that she had the breath to outrun him. He was on her again before she could move. She fought furiously but found herself borne down to the ground. He rose above her, eyes searing their triumph, lips curled in an evil smile. He leaned down toward her and Vickie felt her stomach rise in fear and repulsion.

Then suddenly, a shout stilled him.

"Get off her this instant, you bastard—or I'll pluck your eyes out while you're still living."

Harper's smile faded.

He leapt up because he had to, straddling the earth just above Vickie's head. She tried to struggle up and managed to do so.

There was Jason on Max, staring furiously at Harper from the center of the stream.

He dismounted, striding through the water toward Harper.

Harper drew his sword suddenly from its sheath. Before Vickie could leap away, he had the point aimed against her throat. She stared at Jason with dismay, biting her lip.

"You want to see her ripped from throat to gullet, Reb?"

Jason paused for a moment. He was at least ten feet away. His eyes met hers, glistening silver.

"Take him, Jason!" she cried.

"She'll die!" Harper swore.

Jason eased back. "All right, then, let's negotiate," he told Harper. "You can kill both of us, but my men have surrounded this part of the mountain. Most of yours are dead, or turned tail and ran. Let her go, and I'll give the order to let you pass."

In that instant, Harper eased back just a shade.

Vickie took the opportunity to thrust the blade aside and leap to her feet. Harper swore, and swung his sword.

But too late.

Jason had leapt forward, his sword swinging. Vickie heard the awful clang of steel as their weapons first clashed. Harper fell back. Jason raised his sword again, and his blade crashed down, driving Harper to his knees.

One more crack of Jason's blade, and Harper's blade had flown from his grasp.

"Jesu, mercy!" Harper screamed out suddenly.

Jason looked as if he hadn't heard him. As if his sword would fall upon Harper's head.

"Jason!" she cried his name softly. He held still for a moment, and then turned to her very slowly. He paused just a fraction of a second, and then he smiled and turned toward her.

"Look out! He's got a knife!" another voice from somewhere back in the woods thundered out.

Jason whirled around, dragging Vickie down to the ground as he did so. Harper was pulling his knife from his ankle sheath again, aiming it at them.

Jason was faster. He, too, carried a weapon at his ankle. A gleaming little blade. He had pulled it from the sheath and hurled it for Harper before Harper's blade had left his hand.

Vickie screamed as she watched the blade plunge into Harper's throat. She buried her face into Jason's chest. She heard the man groan, and his gurgling death choke as he fell to the ground.

"Vickie, Vickie!" Jason drawled softly, his fingers working through her hair. "Thank God you're all right."

She looked up at him, shaking her head. She couldn't look at Harper. She couldn't wish any man's death, but that man had meant to cost her her life.

"I'm sorry, Jason! You risked so much for me. He would have killed us both if it hadn't been for—"

She broke off, her eyes widening.

And then they both spoke suddenly, in unison, realizing who had called out the warning to them.

"Gramps!"

With an arm around Vickie, Jason started leading her through the water. Gramps had come there, cutting a very striking figure in his gray cavalry uniform. He had been joined by a number of Jason's men. Vickie looked at them all, smiling as they gravely nodded to her one by one.

Jason walked forward to Gramps. "You saved my life, sir."

Gramps grinned, but his face looked rather gray.

"You saved my granddaughter's life, son. We're even."

"You were fantastic!" Vickie assured him. "Fantastic!"

He nodded, looking at her. "I was, wasn't I? I rather like it here," he told her. Her heart quickened.

Maybe they could stay. She could stay, if Gramps were to stay, too.

She stared at Jason. He returned her gaze, and he seemed to understand the message in it. His fingers curled around hers, and he pulled her close, searching out her eyes.

"Yes!" she said breathlessly. "I think..."

"Colonel, sir?" one of his men said, clearing his throat.

Jason looked quickly to the man who had spoken. "Is everyone here, Jack?"

"Not a man lost, Colonel. Henry back there caught a graze in his thigh, but the bullet went right through. Two minor saber wounds."

"The Yanks?"

Jack shrugged. "Once they lost their captain there, they skedaddled. Which means that we'd best move out, else they'll be all over us like horseflies in August heat. What do you say, sir?"

"Right," Jason agreed. He started for Max, then turned back to Vickie. "You'll ride with me. I guess the Yanks have your horse."

"They don't deserve her," Vickie said softly. Then she looked to Jason's men again, all of them. "Thank you," she told them. "Thank you all so very much."

The one named Jack laughed. "Why, ma'am, it was an honor and a pleasure."

Vickie smiled and Jason set her quickly atop Max. "Well, then, the order is to skedaddle'—" he began, but Vickie gasped, cutting him off.

"Gramps!" she shrieked.

Her grandfather's ruddy cheeks had gone white. He clutched his heart, and pitched forward.

Jason leapt down from Max and hurried toward Gramps. He stared back to Vickie. "He's breathing, his heart is still beating." He stared at her, and then he swallowed hard. They both knew in those seconds that they had to get Gramps back to the twentieth century.

Either that . . . or watch him die.

Jason quickly gave orders to his men. They'd ride back partway together, then Jack would see the rest of the men back to their brigade.

"I have to get this man home—" Jason began to explain.

Jack waved a hand in the air. "Sir, he led us right and proper, he did. We'll send him a prayer."

Jason nodded. He leapt up with Gramps on Dundee.

They moved out in silence, a very solemn party.

Partway back, the company split off and continued their return to camp. Jason led the way to the strange arbor of trees.

"It's closing, you know," Vickie told him hollowly.

He nodded.

"I can take Gramps now," she told him.

He shook his head. "No."

"Jason, I can't let you go through! It's closing. We might not get back and you—" She broke off, feeling a fierce gust of wind tear at her. "Jason, you can't—"

"Vickie, I am coming with you! You can't possibly get your grandfather through this. You haven't the strength."

The wind ripped and tore again. She met his eyes, her own a tempest. "I'm afraid!" she admitted on a whisper, but he seemed to hear it. His horse drew close to hers. "Close your eyes and ride hard!" he commanded her.

There was a whack on Max's rump and she was suddenly flying into the storm.

More than ever, she could feel it. Feel the walls of time closing around her. The fierce wind swirled and funneled, drawing her into its terrifying, mercilessly dark center. As before, mingled with the sounds of the wind, Vickie heard the voices, the howls and chilling moans clearer and closer, more gut-wrenching than ever before. Strange, dark shadows that were human-like forms, and yet horrifyingly unhuman, grasped and reached for her. She heard her name on the wind. They wanted her, wanted to embrace her and make her one of them, imprisoned in this horrid, nowhere place for all eternity. Vickie... stay. Vickie, come, stay....

They stroked her face, tore at her hair. If she opened her eyes, she would see them. Creatures who were barely formed, with empty eyes and pain-filled faces. Neither dead nor living, neither born nor unborn. She could hear their cries on the wind, feel them touching her, closing in on her, grabbing her, clutching her so desperately with their damp, lifeless fingers....

"Ride!" Jason yelled. *"Ride!"*

Jason was at her side, slapping her horse's flanks once again, urging her through.

They burst out into a lighter wind. A keening remained in the trees, but they were through. Her horse reared, and screamed. She maintained her seat until his gait evened out. She gazed at Jason. His face was pale. Vickie couldn't help wondering if he, too, had heard and felt the demon spirits reach for him as he had ridden through.

Gramps hadn't seen or felt any of it. He was slumped over, near death.

"Jason—" she whispered miserably. She was about to lose him again. And maybe Gramps, too, and her heart was filled with desolation for them all.

"We've got to get him to the hospital," Jason said.

"You can't come with me. The passage is almost closed. You'll be trapped in there, Jason. Trapped with those lost souls...."

"Vickie, let's go."

"Then you can't go back."

"Vickie! Let's get moving!"

She lowered her eyes, fighting tears. He wouldn't leave her until Gramps was in the hospital. Then he'd try to go back.

She couldn't seem to fight him on this, to convince him that it was far safer for him to turn back now, while the passageway was still open. She turned and urged her horse forward. They rode down the mountain, heading west, and quickly covered the short distance to Gramps's house. But as Vickie helped Jason carry Gramps inside, she wondered if they had been quick enough.

While Jason made Gramps as comfortable as possible, Vickie called the hospital. An ambulance arrived in minutes. Gramps was swiftly and efficiently whisked away with an oxygen mask over his face and a portable heart monitor attached to his chest.

Vickie and Jason followed in her Jeep. Again, Vickie wished Jason would head back. But she didn't have a moment to spare now to argue with him.

While Gramps was tended to by a team of doctors, Vickie was once again stuck in the admissions office, filling out forms. She prayed under her breath. Poor Gramps. He had to be all right. He just had to.

When she'd finished with the admissions clerk, she joined Jason in the waiting room. He stared at her, not touching her. His eyes fell upon hers.

"I love you," he told her.

She nodded, feeling tears well up in her eyes.

She didn't get to say anything, because someone cleared his throat behind her. It was Sam Dooley, the doctor on call here once again. He looked at them both suspiciously, but didn't say anything—Vickie didn't give him a chance.

She ran to him. "Gramps—will he be all right? Oh, please, Sam! Tell me he's going to be all right!"

Sam smiled at her. "He's fine, Vickie."

"What?" she gasped.

"He's fine. Just a bit of exhaustion."

"No heart attack?"

Sam shook his head. "I'm not sure what he was up to—I'm not sure what any of you are up to!—but he's just got to calm down a bit. No more of this reenacting for him, or he *will* have a heart attack. But this was just a scare."

"Oh, God!" Vickie whispered. "Can I see him?"

"You can even take him home in an hour or so if you want. Just keep him calm, okay? No more running around as if he were really fighting a battle, hmm? He's too old for it, Vickie. Take this as a warning. Make him behave."

"Yes, yes!" Vickie promised. "Thank you again, Sam, thank you. So much." She started to rush through the emergency room doors, but paused, hurrying back to Jason. "Wait!" she begged him. "You just wait this time! Promise. I'll—I'll at least go with you to the . . . door."

Jason nodded, his eyes very dark. "I'll wait," he promised her softly. He added, "We haven't much time."

She nodded, then rushed on in to see Gramps. She cried out and hugged him. "You're okay, thank God! I was so scared, Gramps! But you're going to be all right.'

"It was wonderful, Vickie!" he told her, reaching for her hand. "I wanted to stay."

She swallowed hard for a minute. "But it isn't possible, Gramps. You can't—"

"I'm an old man, and I wouldn't live without modern medicine," he finished grumpily.

"That's right."

His fingers curled around her wrist and his blue eyes were intense. "But you can, honey. You're young. Everything is ahead of you."

There was a knot in her throat and she willed it away, determined to speak lightly. "Gramps, think of it! No movies, no shopping malls, no great rock music. If I had children, no disposable diapers! No, Gramps, you and I will do just fine where we are. But I do have to say goodbye to Jason. I can take you home very soon, so you just rest and I'll be back in an hour or so."

He clutched her hand.

"Gramps—"

He sighed and his fingers eased slowly. "You take all the time that you can, Victoria, you hear? Make him come home with you first. Give him a taste of cold beer and hot chili one more time. You take your time. I'll be just fine."

"The passageway is closing," she said very softly. She tried not to shiver, thinking of the feeling she had had while going through.

"Yes, I know that. But you've got a little time. Make the most of it."

"You're great, Gramps," she said softly. They didn't really have *any* time, but Gramps didn't know that.

"How many old coots like me get a granddaughter like you?"

"Gramps—"

"Go! Time is passing!"

She nodded, and hurried on out again. Jason was waiting. She looked up at him. "I'll drive you back to the house so you can get Max."

"Let's go, then," he said, a husky undertone in his voice.

Vickie's Jeep was parked just outside the emergency room entrance. They drove the short distance back to the house in silence.

At the house, Jason slipped quickly out of the passenger's side of the vehicle. "I never got to learn how to drive this thing. It's amazing. I've seen so many women on the streets with them!"

"We were driving before we got the vote," Vickie said, smiling.

His eyes widened. "*Women* got the vote?" he inquired.

She lowered her head, smiling. "You bet!" she told him softly. "Got something against it?"

He shrugged. "I think it's...remarkable."

She started to laugh, and then she was afraid that she was going to cry. They both started walking toward the house.

Max waited patiently in front of the old oak tree that had stood there huge and gnarled as long as Vickie could remember. She would be willing to bet that if Jason were ever to go by the old house back in his day, the oak tree would be there, drooping and gnarled, just the same.

She was thinking about that tree when they had so little time left together!

She stared at Jason. Felt his eyes on her. She fought the temptation to laugh and to cry again. She swallowed hard. She turned to him, bracing herself for the painful task of saying goodbye. But then Jason surprised her.

"I'd like to come in," he told her softly.

Her conscience told her she should have reminded him of the risk he took in lingering even a moment longer. But she couldn't say a word. Instead, she walked up the porch steps and into the entryway, knowing that he was behind her. She swung around. "This is dangerous. We're playing with your life."

He shook his head. "Damn that tunnel. Damn the war. I can't leave you yet." He was silent for a moment, watching her. "Of all the things that I didn't taste enough, drink deeply enough of, hold close enough...that thing is you. Of all the things I would remember through all time, you are the most incredibly precious."

She threw herself into his arms suddenly. She kissed his lips, and his cheek, and his chin. He returned her hunger, touch by touch, his mouth seeking hers, her throat, her forehead, her lips again.

"You need to go now, Jason. I'm so afraid. That last time, I could feel things holding me, touching me—"

"And I'm not going back until *I* touch you. Just one more time, Vickie, for all time."

She was suddenly lifted into his arms and she stared into his eyes while he carried her surely up the stairs. He knew the right door, and booted it open with his foot. In seconds she was set upon the bed. Fleetingly, she realized it was the first time they had made love on a bed. But comfort was the least of her concerns. She would have made love to Jason anywhere, anytime.

Time was so very precious. She worked upon his buttons while he tugged upon hers. In just seconds their clothes were strewn upon the floor. They knelt upon the bed together, their eyes locked with one another's. Together they reached out, touched one another's shoulders, lovingly, solemnly.

Vickie cried out softly, finding herself borne down to the softness of the mattress, the clean fragrance of the sheets. Next to the coolness of that cotton, his flesh was fire. She stroked and touched him, desperate to memorize the play of his muscles beneath the toned flesh. She ran her fingers down the length of his chest, curling them around the pulse of his flesh. He cried out hoarsely, burying his face against her throat, then kissing her there, rising, starting to kiss, lick and savor the length of her, his tongue trailing through the valley of her breasts, then laving them, one by one, until each nipple was hard and red and peaked and aching. Until the burning streaks of desire begun there reached out through the length of her.

His lips moved from her breasts, trailing over her flesh, teasing her belly, hesitating there, hands beneath her, his caress going lower still. Sweet tremors seized her then, and she reached for him, tugging him back to her, her fingers tense and hungry as they tugged upon his hair.

Her lips hungry as they found his. Savoring his kiss again. She pressed him down beneath her then, taking his lead, trying to cherish every taut inch of him, her kisses traveling over his torso, fingers running lightly over the fine crisp hairs there, her body shimmying even lower against his, until she had taken him in the most intimate of caresses and he raggedly cried out his desire and pleasure. Then, with determined power, he reached for her, brought her beneath him, sunk sweetly inside her.

Moving . . .

Arms and limbs entwined, they rocked together in a timeless embrace. She couldn't bear to be apart from him, yet he forced her a distance so that he could watch her eyes while the richness of desire and need raced through them both. His movement was rhythmic, slow at first, then more urgent. She arched and writhed, desperate to have more of him.

To remember him for all time.

Then even the pain was lost with the pulse that burst upon them both, the driving, blinding desire to find the ultimate crest of pleasure. Climax seized Vickie first, shooting through her like silver arrows. Seconds later, even as she drifted in its exotic sweetness, she felt the sensual explosion of the man above her, heard his cry, felt the tension of his embrace.

Endless time enwrapped them.

Downward, to earth, they came. To the ragged sound of their own breathing.

To the clean softness of the bed beneath them.

Jason eased his weight down beside her. "Sweet heavens above, I can't leave you."

Vickie closed her eyes tightly. The war would go on without him.

But history might change. And not for the better.

She bit her lip, afraid of the lives she might destroy if she did not make him go.

She started to rise. He pulled her back, silver eyes intense upon hers.

"I love you," she said, and kissed his lips. But she tugged upon his hand, and he released her. He watched her while she dressed.

Then he rose. He, too, reached for his clothing. He took her into his arms. "I even love you more for your strength," he told her softly. "I'm sure I forgive you for it."

"And I'm not sure you *would* forgive me if you stayed."

"You could come with me."

"I would—you know that. If it weren't for Gramps."

"Then I'll go alone now—"

"No! I'm coming with you until the very last step!" she swore forcefully.

He smiled. "No sense arguing with a woman these days. You can't win." He tried to speak lightly. They were both quiet as they left the house. He lifted her up on Max, then leapt up behind her.

They started toward the mountain peak where a thick, chilling mist hung like black smoke in the air and an arbor of trees bowed low in a strange arch. The wind rose, pulling at them, coming from all directions at once. The tempest had never been so wild. She had never felt such a sense of fear.

Vickie gasped suddenly as they neared the archway of trees. There, standing just out of the dark passage was Gramps.

"There's a stubborn old fellow for you!" Jason murmured. "I know where *you* get the streak now."

Vickie cast him a quick glare, and he eased her down from Max, dismounting himself. Vickie raced to Gramps. "How did you get here? What are you doing out of the hospital?"

"Dr. Sam Dooley gave me a clean bill of health, Victoria. He said I could go. I saw a friend in the waiting room and asked for a ride—"

"Wheedled some poor innocent into taking you here!" Vickie charged.

He shrugged. "Found Amos Clinton still down by the Yank encampment, and he lent me that old mule of his over there to get up here."

Vickie glanced past his shoulder. There was no mule there, just a tall buckskin horse.

"Sam told you that you had to be careful—"

"Oh, I'm being careful. I just came to say goodbye to Jason, too."

Jason was there now. Gramps reached out a hand. Jason took it tightly. Their eyes met. "You're a fine fellow, Colonel," Gramps told him.

"Thank you, sir. And so are you."

"You'd better say goodbye yourself, Vickie," Gramps warned her, stepping back. "I've been watching the winds and the trees—the whole damned feeling of this place is changing with the seconds now. The door is closing."

"It's closing quickly," Jason agreed, looking down at Vickie.

She swung around and hugged him. He tried to step back. "Vickie . . ."

She nodded, and hugged him more tightly to her. He took her shoulders and pressed her away from him at arm's length, looking into the tumult in her eyes. He was going to tell her something. He was going to tell her that he was afraid to tamper with the future, that someday he was supposed to save Robert E. Lee's life, and if Lee were to die, things might be worse still, just as they had been made so very bad by Lincoln's assassination. He wanted to try and explain so many things.

But the words didn't come.

"Oh, God, Vickie!"

He took her back into his arms again and kissed her passionately. The wind was rising to a wild peak, whipping around them, lashing at them with a wicked fury.

His fingers moved tenderly through her hair. "I love you, Vickie, I love you. I love you so very much. Come with me."

A sob caught in her throat. God, yes! She would give anything to do it. She would brave the those moaning, clasping fingers in the tunnel. What did she have before her? More of those years of loneliness.

Some special years with Gramps, of course, but then . . .

She could live a long, long time. Alone.

"Vickie, I love you. I love you."

"I can't. Oh, God, I would, Jason. But Gramps, he can't live with the hardships of your world, Jason. We've seen that—" Her voice broke off on another sob. "Kiss me again. Just once more."

He kissed her. Long and deeply. While the howling gray wind tore around them, she tasted the heat and the fire and the passion within him in that kiss. She felt the searing warmth of the man, his strength, his tenderness, his love.

Then she broke away from him, tears flooding her eyes. She had to let him go. Quickly. Or perhaps cost him his life. "Goodbye, Jason."

He stood stiffly against the wind. Tall and straight, the ultimate officer. Then he turned, and mounted Max, and started into the arbor.

The voice . . .

Vickie choked down a sob, watching the tempest grip him, toss him. She shuddered, turning back. But suddenly other hands were on her, surprisingly strong hands. She looked up into Gramps's eyes, her own eyes filled with tears.

"What do you think that you're doing, Victoria? Follow him! Quickly, now!"

She shook her head. "I can't leave you—"

"Do I look like a dimwit who can't take care of himself to you? Oh, Vickie, Vickie! I've only so long left, you know."

"Gramps, don't say—"

"What the hell do you think I'm doing here! I had to come to give you a boot through, just in case you didn't see clearly that *you must go.* I'll be fine. It's been a full life, a good life! And yes, I've got a little of it left. Time to argue Liam into the ground. *But I'll be okay.*"

"Gramps, I can't—"

"Vickie! Do you want me spending my days half wishing I were dead because I stood in the way of your happiness? Vickie, let me live out what I've got left, happy myself, knowing that you're loved, that you've found your place. Damn you, granddaughter, go!"

She hugged him tightly. "I can't!"

"You can!" He extracted himself from her. "I love you, Vickie. You've been the best part of my life. Now, go. Make a life for yourself. You won't find your young cavalier again. Go with him. Make him a good wife. And if there is ever any way to do it, you let me know that you're all right, Vickie—that damned thing is almost closed. Go now!"

Once again, Gramps gently pushed her from him. Her face was soaked with tears now.

"Go!" he ordered. "You'll both die if you don't move, and the whole thing will have been for nothing."

"I love you," she told him. "I love you so much."

"*It's closing,* Vickie!"

He walked her to the arborway in the trees. The wind was so strong now that they could barely stand.

"Jason! Jason Tarkenton!" Gramps shouted.

Then he gave Vickie a shove.

She hesitated, looking back, her heart breaking. "Go on!" he cried to her. "*I'll be all right!* Happy as a lark, knowing you're being ... loved! Move, move quickly!''

She closed her eyes, wondering how she could be in such anguish—and yet suddenly very sure of what to do. Gramps was right. She had found her rightful place, with Jason. She couldn't let him go without her.

The world didn't matter. Then, or now. The things that revolved within it didn't matter. Where was the meaning, the light?

Except for love. Love gave life meaning. *Love* was right.

She ran back to Gramps, throwing her arms around him one more time. ''You'll always be with me. In my heart, always.''

''And you, too, sweetheart. You, too. God go with you!''

She nodded, and turned and started to run into the arborway. She paused for a moment, terrified.

The trees lashed in the wind all around her, their branches like spidery hands. Clammy, wet. So chilling. She felt that they wanted to close around her, stop her, cast her back. Hold her there in the limbo, the whirlpool of time, neither in the past nor the present.

''Oh, God!'' she cried out. ''I can't move!''

Faces seemed to whip around her in the clouds. Anguished faces, groaning, crying out. Arms reached out. They were holding her.

The wind! It was the wind, screaming all around her. The space within the arbor was black and circling like some cataclysmic deep-space storm. It was closing quickly. Her hair whipped around her face, blinding her. She could barely see.

"Jason!" She shrieked out his name. There was nothing, nothing!

And then she saw him, a dark shadow upon a dark horse, nothing more for a moment than a dashing silhouette....

"Vickie!" His cry encompassed her. *"Victoria!"* Love and anguish filled his voice.

Then he was before her, reaching down for her, sweeping her up to sit before him atop Max. His lips touched hers so briefly. For they could both feel them now. The hands... holding them. Clinging to them. Trying to keep them from passing through to the other side.

"Hold me! Tightly!" Jason roared. He slammed his heels to Max's haunches. The horse reared, and bolted. Vickie shrieked. The wind made a last tug at her. They were free. While the gray whirlwind tore all around behind them, Jason's gaze met hers with its searing silver, his lips curled into a tender smile, and touched down upon hers.

"We made it. But you shouldn't have come. You risked your life—and you can't go back."

"I couldn't live without you," she whispered.

"Do you think you can live without all those modern inventions—hot dogs, microwaves, cars...?" he whispered.

She smiled, leaning back into the crook of his arm. "You'll have to make it up to me," she told him.

"Hmm," he murmured thoughtfully. Then his lips were on hers again, hungrily. "I'll have to work on that, won't I?"

She nodded, still watching his face with wonder. She stroked the strong planes of his cheeks. "There will be so very much time to work on it together." She paused and gazed deeply into his eyes. "One thing is certain. I love you, Jason."

"I love you, too. So much. For all time, for eternity."

He nudged Max. It was incredibly painful to leave Gramps behind.

It was also wonderful to face the future.

The past.

Whichever.

It didn't matter which. She was facing all the days to come with Jason. Love was leading the way.

His fingers curled around hers as they rode away from the wind-tossed trees, out of the gray swirling mist and into a new life together.

Gramps had just seen them. Despite the whipping winds, despite the deadening gray.

Vickie had stood alone for a moment, slim yet strong, facing the whirling tempest. His head had suddenly grown heavy with fear. It had been too late. They wouldn't make it.

But then he had seen the soldier ride out of the thick shadows, and sweep Vickie up, and away. He had seen them, silhouettes of black against the gray. His granddaughter, held so tenderly in those strong arms, her beautiful face cast back.

And the Reb had kissed her. And for a moment, they had been locked there like that.

They had ridden on quickly. And the swirling mist had closed in their wake.

He closed his eyes for a moment. *Let them be happy. God, please let them be happy!* he prayed.

Then he opened his eyes.

The mist was gone. There was nothing there. Just an arbor of old oaks, the branches barely lifted by a breeze. Nothing more.

He'd let her go. What a stupid old fool. But he smiled suddenly.

He would remember that kiss Jason and Vickie had given each other all the remainder of his days. All of them. And he would be happy.

EPILOGUE

Gramps was climbing up the steps of the house when he saw a car pulling into the driveway. He shaded his eyes from the sun with a hand for a moment, then smiled. It was Vickie's friend, the doctor.

"Hello, there, sir!" the young man called out, stepping from the car.

"Dr. Dooley, nice to see you, nice to see you."

Sam Dooley walked across the yard, taking Gramps's hand, shaking it.

"Didn't know doctors were making house calls these days, though, but it's mighty nice."

Sam grinned. "Well, it's not exactly a house call, though it is good to see that you're looking hale and hearty."

"I feel fine," Gramps told him. "You're a great doc."

"I try," Sam said.

"Come on in, since you seem to be in a frame of mind to chat. Have some chili."

"Thanks."

Sam was slow about getting around to what was on his mind. He was seated with a soda and big bowl of chili before he finally asked the obvious.

"So, have you heard from Vickie?"

Gramps drummed his fingers on the table. "Can't say that I have."

"So she really just ran off with that stranger who came to town for the reenactment, huh?"

"The fellow's name was Jason Tarkenton. Said he came from just past Staunton. I'm not sure where they went, though."

Sam grinned broadly. "You're an old con man, sir."

Gramps shrugged.

"It's hard to believe that she wouldn't have contacted you by now."

"Maybe it's hard for her to get in touch."

Sam nodded. He set his spoon down. "Good chili."

"Thanks."

"There's nothing you can tell me, huh?"

Gramps arched his eyebrows and Sam grinned.

"You came by to question me? The story is pretty simple and . . . and an old one, too. Vickie went away because she fell in love. Are you suspicious, Doc? Suspecting foul play?"

"I do know better," Sam said softly. "I know you wouldn't harm a hair on that girl's head, and you'd give hell to anyone who dared to think of it." Sam paused. "But I did happen to see some mutual friends of mine and Vickie's recently. Karen and Steve. Do you know them?"

"The Yankees?" Gramps said.

Dooley nodded. "Well, they also told me the fellow's name. And I wound up doing some research in some of the old records down in Staunton."

"*Old* records? Why, the fellow didn't look so old to me. I'd guess he was in his early thirties."

Sam's grin deepened, his teeth strong and white against the handsome ebony planes of his face. "You're something, Gramps."

"I'm something? Since when did you become a historian?" Gramps asked.

"I went to medical school. I'm accustomed to reading the fine print," Sam said, laughing. "Besides, I didn't come to ask you anything. I came to let you know something."

He stood up, reached into his jacket pocket, and produced some papers. Gramps saw that they were photocopies of pages from an old record book.

"Go ahead. They're for you."

Gramps picked up the papers. They were church listings, he realized. He saw the name Tanner at the top of the page, and then read lower, coming to Tarkenton.

Tarkenton, Jason and Victoria. Born June 30, 1863, a son, Joseph John. Born April 15, 1865, a son, Axel James. Born September 18, 1868, a daughter, Jeannie Marie. Born May 20, 1872, a daughter, Anne Elizabeth. Born October 17, 1876, a son, Jeremy James.

The next name down the list was Taylor, Henry. He started over, rereading all the Tarkentons.

Gramps looked up at Sam Dooley.

"Thought you might like to see that. Strange coincidence about the name, isn't it?"

"Mighty strange," Gramps agreed. His knees felt a little wavery. Sam was heading for the door now. Gramps started to walk him out.

"Thanks, Dr. Dooley," he said on the porch. He extended his liver-spotted hand. "Thanks. It was mighty kind of you to come by."

Sam nodded. "You take care of yourself. If you need anything, call me."

"And if I can ever do anything for you, sir, you just let me know."

Sam nodded and folded his long body back into the driver's seat of his car.

Gramps waved, smiling slowly as the car disappeared.

"*Five* of them, Vickie!" he said aloud, and started to laugh. "Five of them!" He shook his head. "And not a disposable diaper in sight."

He squeezed his eyes tightly shut. *Well, she must have been—must be?—happy. She's living a full, long life. With a fine man, one who loves her.*

And no matter where you were in time, wasn't that what mattered?

Yes. And it felt damned good to know that he had a whole passel of great-great-grandchildren. Somewhere.

He started to turn to go back into the house, but then his eyes were suddenly drawn by something that seemed to be wedged in the lawn under the old oak tree.

Slowly, curiously, he walked toward it.

There was just a glint of metal. But the metal was attached to something embedded much deeper.

Gramps got down on his knees, and he began to dig. The metal was wedged pretty deep and the digging took some effort. And, after all, he was an old man.

But a persistent old man.

He grew excited as the object began to emerge. A sword. A Confederate cavalry officer's sword. One of the handsomest examples he had ever seen.

Carefully, reverently, he began to wipe the dirt from it. His hands began to shake. He had seen this very sword before.

Only... it was a bit different now.

Right on the blade, near the hilt, it had been engraved. A single tear ran down his cheek. He wiped it away, and he smiled broadly.

"Love you, Gramps. Always, all times. Vickie Tarkenton, September, 1862."

Gramps stood up slowly. He looked to the mountain. "Love you, too, Vickie. Love you, too."

He cradled the old sword to his chest, and walked on into the house.

*   *   *   *   *

And now,
an exciting preview of

SWAMP SECRETS

by Carla Cassidy

Look for SWAMP SECRETS and two other
haunting Silhouette Shadows™ romances
available this month.

And every month from now on, watch for
two new Silhouette Shadows novels,
stories from the dark side of love,
wherever Silhouette books are sold.

CHAPTER ONE

The house sat perilously close to the edge of the swamp, as if fighting a losing battle against the gloom that radiated from the dark, thick woods.

Lindsey Witherspoon slowly drove into the driveway and parked. She pulled a sheet of paper out of her purse and rechecked the address, although there was no doubt in her mind that this was Cindy's house. Only Cindy Mae Clairbourne, with her flair for the dramatic, would choose to live in a house perched at the edge of a swamp.

Lindsey turned off the engine and sat for a moment, looking at the house where she would be staying for the next six weeks. The house itself was huge, a Southern-style mansion with a sweeping veranda that in any other setting would look dignified and stately. However, in this particular place, shadowed by huge pine trees and viewed in the eerie glow of twilight, the house seemed foreboding.

With a small laugh of self-derision, she got out of the car and stretched. Obviously she was more tired from the drive than she'd thought.

She found the key just where Cindy had written it would be, beneath a planter on the front porch. She unlocked the door and pushed it open, greeted by the hot, stale air of a house closed up for several days.

As she walked in, she fought against a sense of unease. Inside, the house was decorated beautifully, but with the heavy wooden shutters tightly closed at each window, no sunlight peeked in to lighten the gloom. She walked from room to room, unlocking and shoving open the wooden shutters, allowing in the jasmine-scented breeze and the sunshine.

She found evidence in the decor that Cindy Mae had changed little from when the two women had been roommates in college. She still apparently had a penchant for blue and peach, as most of the rooms sported the pleasing colors.

Lindsey caught her breath as she walked into one of the bedrooms, deciding this would be the one she would sleep in for the duration of her stay. Sunshine seeped in around the edges of the shutters, casting dancing shadows on the furniture. Lindsey threw open the shutters, raising her face to the sunlight that chased away the shadows and the last of her unease.

The room was gorgeous, boasting a canopy bed covered in a pastel blue spread, and an antique dresser with a large, slightly warped mirror. But it was the French doors that led out to a small balcony that overlooked the back grounds that made Lindsey's decision to claim this room as her own.

She'd always wanted a room with a balcony.

She stepped outside and breathed deeply, smelling the heavy, perfumed scent of strange vegetation, the moist darkness of slow-moving water. It wasn't an unpleasant scent, just different than anything she'd ever smelled before.

The swimming pool was directly below, the water catching the last of the sun. Beyond the pool, landscaped grass intermingled with brilliant-colored flowers. Then the swamp, dark and mysterious, with dead cypress trees rising like giant toothpicks and Spanish moss hanging like shrouds. The swamp was already black with the coming of night, its shadows reaching out to claim all that lay nearby. It was almost as if the darkness didn't come from the fading of day, but was generated from the swamp itself.

Lindsey shivered and wrapped her arms around herself, finding beauty in the scene despite the chill that danced up her spine. She wished she had her camera handy, but it was still packed in the trunk of her car along with her luggage. She'd love to get a shot of the swamp. *There will be time enough for that later,* she thought, once again taking a deep breath.

Cindy's invitation to house-sit while she and her husband, Remy, were in Europe, had been a godsend. Lindsey needed time to think, to evaluate where she was going with her life, what she wanted for herself.

Besides, the swamp would be a perfect place to indulge her passion for photography. She'd always been intrigued by the image of a swamp, although this was as close as she'd ever been to one.

Realizing it would soon be completely dark, she turned and left the balcony. She wanted to get her luggage in before it got too late.

A few minutes later, bags safely deposited in the bedroom, she made herself a drink at the bar in the living room, then turned on the light that illuminated the pool area.

She sank into one of the chaise longues and leaned her head back with a sigh. This six weeks would be good for her. She needed time away from her life back in Washington, D.C., time to lick her wounds and regain her equilibrium. This Louisiana bayou was as good a place as any to have a personal crisis.

She sighed again and moved the handle to recline the lounger. She closed her eyes, intrigued by the night sounds emanating from the nearby swamp. There was no sound of civilization, no automobile noises to shatter the night creatures' whispers.

She must have fallen asleep because she awoke suddenly, for a moment disoriented as to where she was. Night had embraced the area while she slept. No lingering glow of dusk pierced the grounds beyond where the pool light illuminated.

Yet what instantly disturbed her was the silence. The night sounds that had lulled her to sleep were gone, replaced by a quiet so profound it was unnatural. Even the light breeze that had caressed her face before had stopped. It was as if everything held its breath in anxious anticipation.

The hairs on Lindsey's arms rose as if in response to some electrical field, but she knew it was a reaction to the feeling of being watched. She pulled herself up to a sitting position, trying to pierce the veil of darkness that lay beyond the cocoon of light where she sat.

"Hello?" Her voice sounded small, tinny, in the total silence. She squinted, sensing something... someone nearby. "Is somebody there?" She projected more force into her tone and was pleased by the effect, then jumped as a twig snapped and footsteps whispered against the grass.

Fear speared through her as she realized how vulnerable she was, how isolated. The nearest neighbor's house was several miles down the road, and the small town of Baton Bay was a twenty-minute drive north.

She was completely and totally alone. Nobody would hear her scream.

She reached down and grabbed the drink glass she'd brought outside with her. She needed something in her hands, something that could be used as a weapon.

She stood up, adrenaline pumping through her. "Who's there?" Impatience battled her fear as she shielded her eyes, trying to see beyond the glare of the pool lights. "Cindy, is that you?" she called illogically.

"I'm looking for Remy."

The deep voice reached out of the darkness from behind her, surprisingly close to where she stood, making her jump and whirl around in alarm.

He cloaked himself in the darkness, wearing the shadows like a shield of invisibility. The only thing she could discern about him was his height...tall...and his shoulders were ominously broad.

"Who...I..." She was appalled to hear her voice come out as a breathless squeak.

"I'm sorry, I didn't mean to frighten you," he said, but his tone held no note of apology.

"I... You merely startled me," Lindsey exclaimed, tightening her grip on the drink glass, although she had a feeling the fragile glass would be quite ineffective against this man who'd appeared out of nowhere.

"Would you mind stepping into the light? It's rather disconcerting to be talking to a disembodied voice in the dark," she said.

"Certainly." He stepped forward and Lindsey instantly wished he'd remained in the shadows.

The light played on his long hair, trying unsuccessfully to pull a highlight from the unrelenting blackness. His face was one that compelled, all harsh angles and planes unrelieved by any hint of softness. As he took a step closer to her she noticed that his eyes were the color of swamp moss, a deep mysterious green. He was hauntingly handsome, carrying himself with a rigid control that somehow suggested an imminent eruption.

Lindsey unconsciously took a step backward, finding his illuminated face strangely disturbing.

"Remy? Is he here?"

Options battled in Lindsey's head. If she said Remy was home, then what excuse could she give for not going inside and getting him? On the other hand, she wasn't sure she liked the idea of this man knowing she would be alone in the house for the next six weeks. She quickly settled somewhere in between. "Cindy and Remy aren't here right now. Perhaps I can tell them you stopped by, Mr. . . . ?"

"Blanchard. Royce Blanchard." His piercing eyes studied her, again causing a shiver of apprehension to work its way up her back. There was something about him that frightened her. Perhaps if he smiled, she thought. Surely that would relieve some of the harshness, minimize the predatory look in his strange eyes.

"What did you do, Mr. Blanchard? Walk through the swamp to get here?" Lindsey forced a smile to her lips, hoping to pull an answering one from him. She would just feel better if he smiled.

"I didn't come through the swamp. I came from it," he answered, no humor apparent. "I live there."

"In the swamp? Really?" For a moment Lindsey's fear abated as a sudden thought struck her. "Then you must know the swamp very well."

"As much as one can. She guards her secrets well."

Lindsey's gaze went out to the darkness, out where the swamp lay with all its mysteries. He made it sound like a living, breathing entity. In fact, if she listened very hard, she had the feeling she would be able to hear it breathe, feel its heartbeat.

She looked back at him hesitantly, wondering if she was crazy to even consider asking him what she was about to. But who better to guide her through the swamp than a man who lived deep within its center?

Besides, he knew Remy, so surely he was all right. Any man would look sort of spooky in this lighting, she rationalized. In the light of day he was probably very ordinary looking, not spooky at all. This last thought made up her mind. "Mr. Blanchard, I'm planning on going into the swamp while I'm visiting here to take some nature photographs. I could use a guide. Would you be interested?"

He took a step closer to her, bringing with him an earthy, almost herbal scent that was strange, evocative. He stood so near to her she could feel the heat radiating from his body. His gaze seemed to take on a new intensity and he smiled. But the gesture didn't soften his features as Lindsey had hoped; instead it only emphasized their harshness. "It's obvious you're new to the area, otherwise you wouldn't ask such a question."

"Why?"

His features seemed to harden and shadows found the contours of his face as he stared at her. "The last woman who asked me to guide her through the swamp ended up dead."